# Bloody Thursday

**The Brendan Cleary Series, Volume 1**

P.M. Heron

Published by Sirani Publishing Limited, 2018.

BLOODY THURSDAY

**First edition. August 14, 2018.**



Written by P.M. Heron.

**FREE BOOK** – Sign up for P.M. Heron's mailing list and receive a FREE book. Details are at the end. Enjoy **Bloody Thursday**

# Chapter One

BRENDAN WOKE, FEELING groggy. Consciousness caused his head to swirl; even from behind his eyelids it made him feel nauseous. His mouth was dry, and his head pounded. The taste of blood in his mouth, and a swollen, tender lower lip was nothing new. Neither were the stiff finger joints and tight knuckles of both hands. On his back he looked around, wondering what the hell happened last night. Usually a night out in Belfast ended with a kebab and a punch up with somebody outside Turkish Delight – one of Shaftsbury Square's fast food joints. The sudden realisation that he was not in his room made him sit up abruptly. This was a cell – with white walls, a small rectangular window and a stainless-steel toilet in the corner.

He had no idea of the time. His phone, watch and anything that he could use as a weapon had been taken off him when he was signed in. He closed his eyes and rolled over, deciding to go back to sleep. Whatever it was, he'd worry about it later. That was Brendan Cleary: a thirty-seven-year-old with no respect for authority and even worse: no respect for himself.

Some time later he was woken by rattling keys, one of them being inserted into a lock. The hinges of his cell door creaked as it was pulled open. He rolled over to see whoever it was holding the keys to his freedom, pleasantly surprised to see a beautiful lady in a grey trouser suit. She stood around six-foot-tall, with legs that seemed to go on forever. She had a clipboard pressed against her chest, and when she removed her thick rimmed circular glasses, her beauty was only amplified.

'Morning, Brendan!' She stepped into the cell, biting on the plastic tip of one of the legs of her glasses. She stared at him with wide eyes, as if shocked at the sight. 'Hope the head isn't too sore?'

Brendan sat up, rubbing his head where a bump had formed. 'Where are you from? Nice accent.'

She cleared her throat and shifted her stance. 'I'm from London. And thank you for the compliment. But, I'm not here to talk about me. I'm...'

'...here to talk about me and the trouble I'm in?' He finished her sentence. Standing up, he swayed slightly to the right until he found his balance. 'Fancy a coffee?'

He admired the wide hazel eyes sitting nicely above her little button nose. Shoulder length blonde hair draped her perfectly round face, like a set of Laurence Llewelyn-Bowen curtains.

She laughed. 'I don't think you'll be buying anyone a coffee for a very long time.' She turned to leave the cell. 'I'm Agent Lorna Woodward and we have a lot to discuss. So, get ready and meet me outside.'

Exiting the cell, Brendan found his white Nike Air Max on the ground with his phone, keys and a box of twenty Marlborough stuffed inside.

'Follow me. You're being interviewed before your transfer to Maghaberry.' Woodward walked briskly with purpose past the eight other cells towards a set of double doors. Brendan grabbed his stuff and pulled on his footwear.

They passed the police check-in desk at the entrance to the custody suite, paying no attention at all to the officers who'd stopped their conversation to watch them. She opened the door to Interview Room One and indicated for him to enter, following him in as he did so.

Stepping into the room, Brendan made instant eye contact with a middle-aged male. He was borderline obese and looked like someone who didn't feel the need to embrace the free gym memberships or fitness programmes that were freely provided to individuals working for Her Majesty's Services.

'Sit down, Brendan.' The man mumbled under his breath. 'You've gotten yourself into some trouble. You know what you did last night?'

Brendan took a seat. 'I've no idea what I did last night, but I'm sure you're going to tell me.' He looked down at his hands, clenching his left into a fist then releasing it again, feeling how tight it was.

The male agent got up off his seat and strolled around the table towards Brendan. 'Take a look at these.' He threw a stack of photos down on the table.

Brendan looked at the one at the top of the pile. A man wearing a white blood-stained shirt and a neck brace was on a stretcher being wheeled into the back of an ambulance.

'He's in intensive care at the Royal Victoria. He's fighting for his life, thanks to you,' Agent Woodward said, her arms folded. 'We know why you did it, Brendan. We know you buried your granddad...'

'Don't you mention his name.' Brendan slammed his fist down on the table. 'It's because of you lot that our family got torn apart.'

'Be that as it may, your family were involved in the war on these streets. Your father's family were leaders in the Provisional IRA. He was in a position to help the British government and he did so, which was of great benefit to the British...'

'Fuck the British government.' Brendan cut Woodward off for a second time. 'You do know that my mother's older brothers who started up the UDA were ex British soldiers who served here? They even brought other British soldiers into the organisation.' Brendan's face got redder with every word. It was his temper and his self-destructive attitude that had landed him in the fix he was currently in. Now wasn't the time for him to lose his temper.

'What can you tell me about your uncle Bobby?' The male agent asked.

'Nothing good,' Brendan said.

The male agent returned to his seat. Woodward sat next to him. He took the photos back and shuffled through the pile, producing a report from Dr Johns of the Royal Victoria Intensive Care Unit. 'This man is fighting for his life, and you're about to be charged with grievous bodily harm with intent. If he dies, you will be in a lot more trouble.'

Agent Woodward continued. 'Brendan, you've put your home, your family and your friends in danger because of this. You know who this man is?'

'Johnty Burrows.'

The two agents looked at each other. The male leaned over to whisper something in Agent Woodward's ear. He stood up, buttoned his suit jacket and lifted the paperwork. 'I'm Agent Matthew Hughes. I was just a young agent starting out in my career when we brought your dad in to help us...'

'You mean you blackmailed him. Just like you're about to do with me.' Brendan sniggered, folding his arms defensively.

'Okay, let's start again.' Hughes snapped. 'You... Brendan, are likely to spend a good part of your life in prison. Not to mention the danger you and your family will be in if this man dies. However, there is a way out. We could use you. We know your father didn't just pass his DNA on to you. The skill set he acquired at the expense of the British government is now a skill set you have. We could use you, and let's be honest, you could use our influence, too. Unless you like the thought of wasting away in Maghaberry?'

Brendan wanted to help the government that had torn his family apart about as much as he wanted to spend the next ten to thirty years rotting in a cell. He sighed and folded his arms. Shaking his head, he looked at Hughes. 'Get me out of here, and I'll consider helping you.'

'Come with us.' Agent Woodward stood up, her chair screeching behind her. 'We'll get you out. Then you *will* help us.'

# Chapter Two

AFTER A LENGTHY DEBATE with the Assistant Chief Constable, Brendan was signed out of the station. Knowing who Brendan was, the officers were reluctant to let him go, but two MI5 agents appeared to have overruling authority, which to Brendan was all that mattered, as long as he got to breathe free air.

Brendan followed the two agents across the car park towards a black Range Rover Sport that sat in the corner next to the gates. The vehicle was gleaming. It looked as if it had just been driven from the showroom and was more fitting for a convoy chauffeuring heads of state. The SUV had black tinted windows, and judging from the weight of the doors, it was heavily re-enforced. But this wasn't new to Brendan. He grew up in a multi-million-pound house on the outskirts of Belfast, overlooking the city. The family estate that sat proud, like the man-made king of Cave Hill mountain, was complete with a driveway full of luxurious cars.

Brendan climbed into the back seat. Agent Woodward got behind the wheel while Agent Hughes took the front passenger seat. As they waited for the security barrier to lift, Brendan's line of sight followed a commercial jet lowering it's altitude. He watched it, wishing he was on one going in the opposite direction.

'Where are we going?' Brendan lit up a cigarette and lowered the window.

'We're going for a drive through the streets you call home,' Woodward said. 'Play your cards right and you'll be able to walk them again soon.'

They cruised up the catholic Falls Road of West Belfast, turning right onto the Springfield Road, then through the gates of the notorious Peace Wall onto the protestant Shankill Road. This eyesore of corrugated iron – some parts reaching eighteen feet in height – was erected in 1969 at the beginning of "The Troubles" as they became known worldwide. Foreign visitors to the city couldn't believe that the two most extreme places in the city – The Falls and The Shankill – were within touching distance.

Brendan, however, had grown up being somewhat sheltered no matter what side he was on. His father – Damien Cleary Jr – had two older brothers who were members of the Provisional IRA's Army Council and had spent a lot of their time during the early 1970s in Dublin challenging and eventually overthrowing the OIRA for It's failure to protect the catholic areas of Belfast and Derry.

In a city so dangerous, Brendan was heavily protected by this organisation. But, to make his bloodline even more controversial, Damien Jr fell in love with and married Brendan's mother – Vanessa Moore – who had three brothers whom were former British soldiers who went on to start the UDA in 1971.

After being framed by the state for murder, Brendan's father was blackmailed into becoming an agent for British Intelligence. Damien's ties to both organisations allowed him to get close without any questions.

Brendan felt like a tourist of his home city as they cruised south on the Shankill Road, towards the Crumlin Road. Woodward turned and looked at Brendan. 'You want to help this community?'

'I want to go and get a fry, I'm starving,' was Brendan's response.

'Well, you can sit back there and act the hard man if you want, or you can act like a man, and make a decision that will better not only your life, but the lives of both communities in Belfast.'

'What do you expect me to do?' Brendan flicked the cigarette out the window and folded his arms defensively as the Range Rover cruised past the Mater Hospital where he was born. 'I'm not my father. I can't do what he did, and why would I want to? He got killed because of the position you put him in.' He spat out the window.

'Your family got torn apart because they were involved in the IRA and the UDA,' Woodward said.

'UDA? Your government helped breed it. Kept it a legitimate organisation until 1992. Colluded with it's members. Supplied them with guns and intel on Catholics. Get off your high horse, love.'

'Screw this, we'll take him back to the station. Let him rot!' Woodward said.

'Both of you shut up!' Hughes shouted, directing Woodward to pull over behind the Orange Hall which sat just off the Carlisle Circus roundabout. 'He's not going anywhere, Lorna. We need him.' He took his glasses off and rubbed his eyes with his knuckles. Lifting his head, he turned and looked at Brendan with reddened eyes. 'Look, Brendan. I agree. The government, the people I've given my entire life to, was just as bad as the paramilitaries. They certainly did nothing more than create more unnecessary bloodshed. On both sides.'

'We've taken a great risk releasing you today, Brendan,' Woodward continued. 'It's safe to say, after we tell you what we're about to, we'll both face longer stretches than you.'

Hughes lowered his window and pulled out a twenty box of Regal Filter. 'Here.' He handed one back to Brendan, then offered one to Woodward. She quickly refused and said she was trying to give them up. He lit Brendan's, then looked out through the windscreen as a white police Landrover drove past, turning off in the direction of the Antrim Road. 'So many unnecessary lives lost in this bloody place.' He lit his own cigarette and took a long draw, blowing the smoke out the window. His body the jerked. Blood splattered all over the window and he fell forward, his limp body being supported only by the seatbelt.

'Jesus Christ!' Woodward ducked as her window was struck, followed by her seat being pelted, bits of leather flying into the air. Brendan dove down across the back seat as the car was riddled with bullets. Woodward put the car in gear and stomped on the accelerator. The car sped off, back onto the roundabout, down towards the intersection that connected the traffic in and out of the city. Turning left, they headed north bound on the M2 motorway.

'What just happened?' Brendan shouted, looking at Agent Hughes' corpse slumped across the passenger seat.

'How did they know we were here?' Woodward thought out loud as the car pulled up at the traffic lights leading onto the motorway.

'Who are *they?*' Brendan shouted.

Woodward acted as if she was still being pursued. As the light went from amber to green, the SUV rocketed up to seventy mph within seconds. 'They, Brendan are the government we work for.'

'Okay, and why are they assassinating their own agents?' Brendan hung over the driver's seat, looking at Woodward's trembling hands playing around with the radio.

'I need to get you out of here. We need to find somewhere to hide. They could be watching us. Christ, they could be tracking this car. We'll need to ditch it and get another.'

# Chapter Three

TWENTY MINUTES AND seventeen miles later, they pulled off the M2 motorway at the junction for Antrim. Merging onto the dual carriage way heading into the town, Woodward finally reduced the speed to sixty mph. The passing fields, and scattered farms were gradually replaced by the steel fenced concrete blocks of warehouses, factories and car dealerships. Three hundred yards from the end of the dual carriage way towards the Greystone roundabout, Woodward spotted a police patrol vehicle pulling onto the roundabout from the opposite side. She took the final left before reaching the roundabout, pulling into the industrial estate. The car slowly came to a halt outside the gates to the local council dump which merged onto a deprived looking grass patch. At the other end of the field were a bunch of houses. Houses meant cars. Cars meant getting away. In their current race for survival, that was all that mattered.

'We'll ditch this here and go in there,' Woodward said, pulling her dead colleague's pistol out from inside his jacket. 'We'll need another car.' She gestured across the patchy field that was dressed with a thirty foot wide and twenty foot high stack of blue and red wooden pallets. The top of the stack had three Irish tri-colour flags and a Republic of Ireland football banner.

'You're asking me to be involved in car theft now?' Brendan said. 'And you're asking me to go into a loyalist estate after what happened last night?' Brendan was aware that Burrows, the person he almost killed the night before, was a leading loyalist paramilitary. Some seen him as a loyalist godfather. To others he was the operating commander of the LVF in North Belfast and had a few thousand strong combatants at his command. The housing estate they were about to enter was a loyalist stronghold. With it's preparation for the annual Twelfth of July parades well underway, people would be feeling extra tense when it came to their communities.

'I'm afraid, we've got bigger things to worry about than the LVF being out for your blood,' Woodward said. 'And call me Lorna. Agent Woodward is too official.' She handed him Hughes' pistol. 'Like it or not, we're both targets now. God, how did they get on to us.' She pulled her suit jacket off, grabbed her handbag and jumped out of the car. 'Here, hold these.' She handed her bag and jacket to Brendan.

Brendan stood at the front of the Range Rover watching as she went to the boot and took out a can of fuel. He watched as she doused the car with her colleague's corpse inside. She even used Hughes' own lighter to turn his final resting place into a blazing inferno.

'He meant nothing to you?'

'There's no time to be sentimental. If you don't want to be next, you'll learn to leave everything you've ever loved behind.'

'The person I loved the most was buried yesterday.' Brendan thought briefly about his grandfather, Damien Cleary Snr, the man who'd taken over in the absence of Brendan's father. A man feared by many in Belfast. Loved by a lot people, hated by just as many.

They made their way across the field. Tyre tracks imprinted in the mud. Marching directly passed the mountain of pallets that would soon be blazing as much as the Range Rover behind them, they saw a spray-painted slogan which read: *Damien Cleary Snr... Burn In Hell!*

Brendan stopped and looked at it, studying it. A lawn mower was being guided over a garden in one of the houses they were heading towards. He followed the hum of the engine. The gardens were surrounded by a six-foot wooden fence.

He kicked the gate open, snapping one of the panels. Spotting a can of petrol sitting beside a brown garden waste bin, he went for it, without any consideration for the owner of the garden. The man's jaw dropped as he watched Brendan grab it.

'Hold on a second, where do you think you're going with that?' the man shouted, dropping the handle of the mower. He was shocked, not sure what was happening.

Brendan made the guy aware of the pistol in his hand and said nothing else. He ran out of the garden and back across the field towards the stack. He emptied the can out onto the base of the construction, grateful there was little more than a breeze.

'Lighter.' He looked at Lorna who was standing with her arms folded. She tossed him the lighter even though she obviously disapproved. He grabbed a plank of wood he'd soaked and used it to start the bonfire. 'You can be shot for something like this.'

Six men, one of them the owner of the fuel, walked towards them. Three had baseball bats, two had claw hammers and one looked like he was so tough that he didn't need a weapon. Just his fists.

'Brendan, we've gotta go. Move.'

One of them threw their bat. It went spinning past Lorna, brushing past her head. She pulled her pistol out and pointed it at them. Brendan did the same.

Brendan fired two shots into the ground at their feet. 'Don't move another step closer. Trust me this isn't a good time.'

'Cleary, you're dead, mate!' shouted the one who didn't have a weapon. 'Within twenty-four hours you'll be sleeping next to your scumbag grandad.' He looked at one of his baseball bat wielding mates and laughed, but that quickly dissolved when Brendan put a bullet in his leg. He dropped to the ground.

'Brendan!' Lorna shouted. 'Come on, hurry up.' She ran across the field towards the row of houses. He followed. The other side of the houses was a closed off street. A dark blue Subaru Impreza sat idling, the keys in it.

'Thank you very much,' Brendan said. 'This'll do nicely. Not like they can report it stolen.'

'They definitely can't,' Lorna said, as she looked under the passenger seat. She pulled out a handgun and what looked like a kilo of cocaine.

Brendan jumped in behind the wheel.

'Let's see what this thing can do then,' Lorna said. She fastened her belt.

They exited the estate, passing a *Welcome to Newpark* sign.

'You know where to go?' Lorna said, lowering the window.

He nodded and hummed in agreement, jumping up through the gears. He raced down the road until he reached the Belfast Road, leading to the Seven Mile Straight country road towards the city.

'We've gotta hide somewhere until it gets dark. Then we can figure out what the hell we're going to do,' Lorna said, shaking her head. 'Christ, what the hell's just happened?'

'Don't ask me. You dragged me out of the Grosvenor Road station to do God knows what, and we end up having the car riddled with bullets and your partner's brains splatted all over the window.'

She didn't say anything, just brought her trembling hand up to her face, massaging her forehead.

Twenty minutes later, Brendan pulled off the Seven Mile Straight onto a mile-long driveway that led up to a modern house. 'Don't worry,' he said, looking at the concerned expression on Lorna's face. 'It's my uncle's house, but he spends more time in Galway than he does up here.'

The Impreza roared up the gravel covered driveway, around the side of the house to the back. Brendan parked it outside the double garage. He jumped out and ran over to a flower bed that ran along the side of the garage. Lifting a stone in amongst a bunch that were scattered around the soil, he pulled out a key and returned to the car. 'Let's go, we can hide out here for a while.'

After de-activating the alarm, they entered the luxurious house through the kitchen and went into the living room. The magnolia walls were covered in art that Brendan's family didn't seem the type to collect.

'Go get a shower, wash that blood off you,' Brendan said, as he went to the cupboard below the stairs. He pulled out a cream towel and threw it to Lorna. 'You could wash your clothes, but I doubt you'll want to wear them again.'

'We need to burn any evidence of what happened.' Her voice trembled as she turned and walked back into the living room. Brendan followed her. Sitting down beside her, he noted her glazed eyes and pale face.

'God what a mess.' She looked at him. 'Give me a cigarette.'

'Thought you were quitting?' Realising it wasn't the time to joke around, he lit one up and gave it to her, then lit one for himself. 'So,' he said, as he exhaled a long draw of smoke. 'You know what, I don't want this.' He jumped up and stubbed the cigarette out. 'What am I involved in?'

Lorna exhaled smoke, and got up from the sofa, following Brendan's example. 'Cancer sticks.' She sat back down again. 'Agent Hughes had discovered some classified information that goes right to the top of the British government. Information that would cause our government to lose all it's credibility if it were to get out.'

Brendan sounded intrigued, but not surprised. 'You mean the British government's done some dodgy stuff?' He laughed. 'You're not telling me anything I don't already know.'

'What if I told you the British government that was in power in the late 1960s wanted the troubles to start and wanted the IRA to force a referendum with a majority vote in favour of a united Ireland.'

'I'd say you're full of shit! Why would they?'

'Because the Labour government at the time couldn't care less about the troubled six counties of Ireland. Simply put,

Britain doesn't want Northern Ireland and all it's baggage. But of course, they must create a way to get rid of this province without looking like the bad guy.'

'So, where do you and the late Agent Hughes come into this?'

'My father was killed by an IRA sniper when I was a baby. I grew up hating the organisation that took my father. When I found out the British government was just as much to blame, and planned to re-start a similar scenario, I thought, I don't want another person to grow up with what I had to grow up with.'

'And our dead friend who helped you get me out of custody?'

'Agent Hughes had worked for British Intelligence for as long as I've been alive. He dedicated his life to Her Majesty's Service,' Lorna shook her head. 'And to be taken out the way he was today, well, that just shows you how ruthless they are.'

'So, what happens now - and what did you expect me to do?'

'Your father left behind not only a son with the same heart and skill set as he, but also information. Tangible information about what he was forced to do. If this got out it would be disastrous. Some very powerful people, pillars of British democracy would be incriminated. Now the British government has done kind of a reverse role play by sending undercover agents into both organisations to help them re-build their armies ready for a re-start of violence. The CIRA and RIRA have always wanted to continue their war with the British, and now they're getting not only the information and motivation they need, but also money to fund their campaigns.'

'And this is all just to make Northern Ireland ungovernable again, so the British can give it up?' Brendan shook his head. 'I don't know what information I'm supposed to have. My father never gave me anything. He's been missing, presumed dead for the past seven years.'

Lorna just looked at him. A suspicious look on her face, as if she was searching for truth in Brendan's words. But he had no reason to lie.

# Chapter Four

AFTER A SHOWER, BRENDAN changed into the best fitting clothes he could find. A black hoodie, dark jeans and black boots. It was helpful that he and the owner of the house were a similar size. His uncle had many female companions come stay with him, so it wasn't long before Lorna found a pair of cream jeans, brown shoes and a pink blouse.

Brendan cooked them a chicken pasta bake that he'd found in the fridge.

'When can we expect your uncle to come back?' Lorna said, as she set the table. 'We need to stay invisible. It's going to be very dangerous for anyone we come into contact with.'

'Then we better make sure we don't get caught. But where do we start?' Brendan watched the pasta bubble at the surface. He pulled down the oven door and sniffed as he lifted the dish off the top shelf. 'And Bobby won't be back for a while.'

'We were going to get you to go back to both organisations, using your granddad's death as your reason to become reckless. This was with the hope you could sniff out the British agent that's working within the organisations.' Lorna looked at Brendan as his eyes narrowed. His jaws clenched. 'I'm sorry, Brendan,' she said, remembering his grandfather had only been buried the day before.

He placed the dish on the centre of the table and sat down facing her. 'There's nothing you could have done to help him.'

He looked at her, shaking his head. 'This is insane. Your boss, an intelligence agent is dead and we're lucky to be alive. Just process that for a second: a high-ranking British agent has just been disposed of like he was a family pet. Agent Woodward,' he cleared his throat. 'Lorna, this goes way above our heads.' He lifted a glass of water. 'I've no idea how to process this. I mean, what the hell just happened?'

'Unfortunately, we've just become targets of the state. And something very big is about to happen over here. We need to find out who's dealing with who on the ground, who exactly is meeting with the leaders of these groups. Then we gather some evidence. I've heard there's an arms shipment coming in somewhere.'

'If anyone's running things on the C.I.R.A side, it'll be Malachy Collins. He's been the head since the group started up again. He lives down in the Twinbrook estate over in the west of the city. But if we're going to get close to them, we'll need information from someone.'

'Can we find someone trustworthy?'

Brendan looked around the room.

'You want to use your uncle? You know it's dangerous?'

Brendan shook his head and shrugged off the comment dismissively. 'He's not my blood uncle. He married into my family. But he always followed my father and grandfather around thinking he was the dog's balls. I'm guessing now with them dead, he'll latch onto anyone he thinks can help him maintain his "hard-man" persona.'

'What's he doing in Galway?'

'I'd bet my life he's down there selling guns to the local scumbag gangsters. Trying to fund the CIRA and it's operations.'

'How do we get in touch with him?'

Brendan pulled his phone out. 'I'm calling him now. Keep quiet.' He put the phone on loudspeaker. Listening to it ring, he looked at Lorna, helping herself to the food. 'I meant what I said in the cell this morning, you're one beautiful lady.' He smiled at her.

'Charmer.' She filled her plate, then his.

Someone answered. 'Brendan, what the hell's going on up there? I've heard you've taken Burrows out? What did you do that for?'

'Bobby, he made a joke about granddad, and only hours after he was buried. What did he expect to happen?'

'It's that temper that's always gotten you into trouble,' Bobby said. 'Where are you now? Do you need money to get out of the country?'

'I'm at your house. I want to get back in on the action again. I'm not making any money. Not like I can just go and get a job!' Brendan looked at Lorna, staring at her phone, her mind elsewhere. 'I don't know who I can trust, Bobby.'

'Okay. Well, it seems you may have come at the right time,' Bobby said. 'Malachy said he's got *big* news regarding another campaign, one that will make the Provos' campaign during the troubles look like kid's stuff.'

Brendan looked at Lorna. Her face lit up and she was again, present in the room. She whispered for him to keep him talking.

'What do you mean, Bobby. What's happening?'

'He didn't go into detail. He just said he was meeting with someone about a major arms deal tomorrow.'

'Where are they meeting? I want to join in on that conversation.'

'You didn't get this from me, okay? I'll get shot!'

'I'm not stupid, Bobby!' Brendan said, looking at Lorna.

'They're meeting in Frames Snooker Hall, in the pub part on the ground level. He seemed excited about this meeting, Brendan. He was talking about re-writing history.' He sighed. 'For Christ's sake, I thought the troubles were over. Dead and buried forever.'

'Okay. I'll speak to you tomorrow. Are you staying in Galway for a while? I'll maybe come down and say hello.'

'Aye, I'll be down here for a few weeks at least.'

'Okay. Do you have any money stashed up here at the house? I'm skint!'

'Check up the stairs in my chest of drawers. There should be a Bank of Ireland card. I'll text you the PIN.'

Brendan hung up. Looking at Lorna, he smiled. 'Want to go shopping get some supplies?'

'Why not?'

'The city-side shopping centre will do the job.'

'Do we have other transport here?'

'He should have a couple of cars in the garage.'

Brendan looked across the room. 'He usually keeps them up there.' He got up and walked over to the mantelpiece. Grinning, he waved the keys to an Audi. 'Let's go and see if it's there.'

They exited the house, through the kitchen and out the back door. They ran along the garden path towards the garage block, getting pelted with raindrops the size of marbles. Rolling up the door closest to them, a gunmetal grey Audi A8 beeped when he pressed the unlock button.

'That'll do the job.' Brendan dropped the door again.

'Let's go and have our dinner, then we can go get ready!'

# Chapter Five

BRENDAN AND LORNA LEFT Bobby's house at three thirty. As the vehicle roared up the Seven Mile Straight, the narrow, winding road that gave a picturesque view of what the world viewed Ireland as being like, green in abundance, Lorna put the radio on. Cool FM, a local radio station was saturated with news about a burnt-out Range Rover found in the Newpark Industrial Estate with the body of a middle-aged man inside. Police were asking for witnesses. Strangely, the residents who had the altercation with Brendan and Lorna hadn't mentioned seeing them.

'Why haven't we been reported?' Brendan said, as he pulled off the country road, turning left city bound. 'Obviously, we were seen in the area and shouldn't have been there. For Christ's sake, I put a bullet in one of their legs.'

'Perhaps our new friends have things to hide and didn't want the police sniffing around.'

'And, or, they want to take care of us themselves.' Brendan rammed the gearstick into higher gear with an aggressive shove as the vehicle climbed the hill, leaving farmhouses in the distance.

On the way over the mountain into Belfast, the entire city could be seen, the divided estates. A city that still bore the scars of it's violent past. And now Brendan could soon be in possession of information that would place a question mark directly above the British government. They were about to re-write the recent history of Ireland. And perhaps more importantly save countless lives, if a return to violence was the goal of the British government. As laughable as it was, something was going on.

'Where are you taking us?' Lorna said, lowering the passenger window.

'The shopping centre at the old docks area.' He turned into a neighbourhood lined with Irish tri-colours. Passing through the neighbourhood, he spotted graffiti on the wall that said *RIP Damien Cleary*.

'Looks like the people of Belfast have an opinion on your family.'

'Tell me something I don't know.' Brendan pulled into the shopping complex. He shut the engine off. A silence fell over the car. He looked at Lorna. 'I've no fucking idea what we're doing here.'

She smiled. 'Come on, we'll figure it out.' She opened the car door and got out. 'Either that or we're dead.'

Walking towards the shopping complex, Brendan put on a black baseball cap, pulling the peak down over his face. 'I feel like a bloody thug.'

'You look like a bloody thug!' She joked.

After an hour of changing their appearance, they went back to the car. Brendan received a message from Bobby. The message regurgitated the "big" meeting in the usual place. All CIRA and RIRA leaders were to be there, without exception. But before the big meet, there was a more formal meet with some suits from London.

'If we get there early, it'll stop from attracting any attention to us,' Lorna said. 'I want to find out who in MI5 killed Hughes and wants us dead.'

'Talk about doing something to sober up!' Brendan joked without humour. He started the car, feeling comfortable in his new Lonsdale tracksuit. 'We need to get petrol, but we'll use one of the stations up in Glengormley, the next town. I don't want to be here longer than I need to be. People from the Newlodge area will recognise this as Bobby's car.'

Exiting the shopping complex, the time was four thirty. Just as the afternoon rush hour of manic workers scrambled onto the M2 motorway northbound, leaving the city and their work lives behind for the day.

Glad to have heavily tinted windows, Brendan kept the vehicle in first gear as it crept along in the queue of traffic up the motorway. Passing the train station on the left, the traffic began to speed up. Slowly, the car went from second gear, to third, into fourth, then fifth, and finally into sixth as the congestion began to thin out and the wind began to come in through Lorna's window.

Three miles up the road, Brendan indicated to come off. The slip road took them into North Belfast's Glengormley area. After a slight battle to get on the roundabout, the car exited onto the Antrim road, and followed three taxis for another one hundred and fifty yards. Indicating to go right, Brendan entered a Tesco filling station.

Pulling up to pump five he filled the Three litre Quattro. He realised that the fancy car he was driving came at the expense of others misery. But what the British government was planning would cause much more misery. He was unsure how he and a lady he'd known for less than twenty-four hours were going to stop it. But at least he was free, not rotting in Maghaberry Prison.

In the car, Lorna was biting her nails. For a second time, he regarded her beauty. This beautiful lady who'd just lost her partner and mentor was now out in the middle of nowhere with someone she'd seen lying in a heap on a cell mattress no more than a day before; now on the run from the government she'd given her life to. She looked vulnerable. And he was drawn to it.

'We'll figure it out,' he told her. 'Out of everything my father taught me, the main thing was that you're not done until your heart stops beating. Is your heart still beating?'

She laughed. 'I think so, otherwise I'd be slumped against the window going cold.'

'Well then, we're not done yet.' After paying the sixty pounds to fill the German beast, he jumped back in. 'Let's go and grab something to eat, I'm starving. What do you fancy?'

'Fish and chips? Although, Irish fish and chips can't be as good as those in London.'

'I wouldn't be so sure about that.' He smirked, pulling out of the petrol station and back onto the M2 north bound, both agreeing a little more distance from Belfast was best.

# Chapter Six

BACK AT BOBBY'S HOUSE, Brendan went through his uncle's secret stash of guns; a mixture of handguns and rifles well known to be the preferred weapons used by the Provisional IRA during it's armed campaign against the British state, the loyalist paramilitaries and the RUC (the local police force).

Going through a black sports bag, he came across a black bin liner full of photos. Kodak albums from when he was a boy. He took out a photo from the bunch. His holy communion. He cast his mind back to that day. At the evening dinner, he remembered his father having to leave.

'You alright?' The question brought Brendan back into the room. 'What is it?' Lorna sat on the bed beside the pile of weapons, surely destined to wreak havoc on the already tainted streets of Belfast.

'I remember this day as if it were yesterday.' He handed Lorna the photo. 'He always disappeared, but eventually came back.' He cleared his throat. 'Now I know why he disappeared for good. He had no balls.'

'Perhaps he kept you and your mother out of it because he knew the danger it would have put you both in.'

'He should have told us. We could have run, together. Went with him.' He threw the bag down on the ground. 'Bastard.'

'Jesus, Brendan you don't know the half of it,' Lorna said, sounding fed up.

Brendan looked at her, shocked. Scanning her face for authenticity in her comment. 'Then fill me in.'

'Everything your father did was for you and your mother. He was framed for murder by the British government. Not because the government wanted him behind bars, but because they wanted to blackmail him into becoming the person he eventually became. They wanted him to gather information on both the IRA and the UDA, but they started to use him for more: global intelligence gathering. He could have backed out at any time, but the thought of rotting in a prison and being separated from you and your mother was too hard for him to bear. So, he decided to give the British government what they wanted. Not a person alive could have done what he did. He's a fucking legend in British circles. But in the end, he became an agent with so much classified information that he was too valuable to them.' She sighed, took the photo off Brendan. 'Everything he did, he did for you.'

'He died because of them.' Brendan looked down at the photo.

'I'm sorry, Brendan.' She grabbed his hand.

'It's not your fault.' He squeezed her hand. He had a flashback to when his father had taken him to a place, somewhere he'd always called their special place. A training camp built with his own hands. In Donegal. A place where Brendan spent every summer of his teen years. This was where Damien Cleary turned young Brendan into the man he was today; a person with much mental toughness. An unbreakable mind. A focus so precise, it would be impossible for Brendan to be broken.

Kind of like a Pitbull with lock-jaw, that simply didn't have the ability to let go. Yet, until now, Brendan never had any use for it. Perhaps his father had seen it all coming and thought if he were to lose his life because of it, then his only son would have the skill set to put right all the wrongs he had done. 'Now it makes sense.' He looked Lorna. 'My training. All those terrible, painstaking summers I spent in Donegal when I'd rather have been with my mates.'

'What training?'

'He had a strict schedule he made me stick to. There was a classroom where I'd learn about world affairs, with foreign language and policy. Irish and British history. The British and Irish legal systems. How to recognise the most commonly used weapons: their bullets, bombs, and bomb making equipment.' He chuckled, looking thoughtfully at a scar on his hand. 'But my favourite was the gym and shooting range. He taught me martial arts – four different arts to black belt. He taught me how to shoot, from close and long range. He taught me tactical knowledge. He used to joke about how the British government's training would one day come back to haunt them. But I never knew what he meant. I thought it was just some little joke he kept to himself.'

'So, you're telling me you have the knowledge and training that he possessed?' Lorna smirked, her eyes wide. 'I'd bet my life that there's information there, perhaps he kept it there for you.'

Brendan didn't reply. He gazed at her, his stare becoming more intense. 'You're really beautiful. How about you let me buy you dinner and take you on a date after this?' He moved his face in closer to hers.

She turned her face to the left, causing his lips to land on her cheek instead of the intended target. 'Maybe after.' She smiled. 'Come on, Prince Charming. We should make tracks.' She picked up the photograph of him making his holy communion. 'Here, keep this with you!' She shoved it into his jacket's pocket.

This time Lorna drove the Audi. A new Samsung Galaxy allowed them to have some access to the internet and news. A news report stated that the body found in the black Range Rover in the Newpark Industrial Estate was that of a leading loyalist paramilitary. The police hoped this was not going to result in a "tit for tat" spate of retaliation shootings.

Brendan looked at Lorna. She glanced back at him, smirking. They both knew what the other was thinking.

'Don't always believe what you hear on the news,' Lorna said, as she pulled up to a crossroad at the end of the Seven Mile Straight. 'You know they won't let us live, Brendan?' She looked at him.

'They can't afford to,' he said, shaking his head as he saw an armoured police car passing them. 'So, before they get us, let's finish them. We're dead if we don't. And keep your distance from that car. The chances are they'll know this is Bobby's car and the last thing we need is to be pulled over.'

# Chapter Seven

LORNA WAITED FOR ANOTHER two cars – a grey Vauxhall Astra and a blue Ford KA to pass before pulling onto the road that would lead them down the Crumlin Road into the North Belfast area. The streets looked relatively normal compared to the past. Less IRA and UDA graffiti marking each groups' territory. No *Fuck the Pope, Up the UDA* or *Fuck The Queen, Up the RA* slogans gracefully sprawled across residential fences and walls. No burnt-out cars and shops.

Northern Ireland, although still trying to repair the damage from the previous two generation's war, looked like any city in England, Scotland or Wales. Not perfect, but normal.

Arriving at the bottom of the Crumlin Road at the roundabout to Carlisle Circus, they both looked at each other. He checked his pistol was close by. A feeling of returning to the scene of the crime was cast over the car. It was only five forty-five; the meeting in Frames was seven thirty, so they didn't need to rush. Lorna was new to Belfast, so Brendan guided her through the red-bricked Victorian streets of the city until they arrived just outside the club.

They both tasted a bitter sensation of dark humour at the fact she'd just pulled over facing the snooker hall. The adjacent building was the Belfast Telegraph newspaper office.

'Wonder what bull-shit story they're conjuring up in there,' Brendan said. 'Better if we don't park here, take a left and we'll park around the corner.'

They left the vehicle in a bay outside a Chinese takeaway called "The China Garden". It was directly around the corner from Frames, close enough to get to in a hurry, but not so close that they could risk bumping into someone. With their puffy coats on to hide their fully loaded pistols, and baseball caps pulled down over their faces, they made their way into the bar part of the snooker club, passing a black Ranger Rover Sport, almost identical to the one Lorna had sent into a raging inferno with Hughes inside.

'Nice suits,' Brendan whispered in Lorna's ear as they walked past the SUV, a group of middle aged men wearing pasty looking grey suits. The last of the three to get out of the vehicle wore a black overcoat and carried a leather bag with what looked like a laptop inside. He had that look. That untouchable look of a man of power. A man who perhaps didn't often, if ever, get his hands dirty.

Brendan and Lorna walked into the main bar area. Walking straight to the bar, Lorna asked for a cola and a fizzy orange. Brendan kept his head down. Having a well-known face in Belfast, both he and his family had difficulty moving around without being recognised. And now he was supposedly undercover he was certainly not about to make eye contact with anyone other than the beautiful London-born lady who was his pretend dinner date.

She led the way towards a booth in the corner, next to the door.

'Enjoy your coke - and since we're meant to be on a date you should at least smile!' Brendan joked.

'Don't flatter yourself, handsome.' She looked directly at him while sucking through her straw.

'God, you may as well be a teenage girl, blowing bubbles with pink chewing gum!'

She was quick to hush him as a group of five entered. 'Where do I know him from?' She gestured at one of the older guys. He was tall and thin, his spindly arms looked drenched in his blue Rangers jersey.

'That's my friend Jonty's brother AKA the commander of the Shankill Road C Company,' Brendan breathed into her ear.

'If he spots us it'll erupt in here.'

'Fuck him, and fuck Jonty!' Brendan fumed.

They watched as the five ordered pints, then piled into the booth next to them, sounding in high spirits.

The suits from outside in the Range Rover entered the pub and walked straight to the bar. The bar man – who was about Brendan's age - pointed them in the direction of the five.

Brendan turned his back to them and faced Lorna. Moving in for a kiss, he hoped she'd get the meaning behind it. Luckily she did, and he finally got a kiss from her.

She separated, slowly. 'Don't be getting any ideas, you!' she said, the tip of his strong nose touching her button nose.

'What?' He grinned. 'I've taken you out on a date, bought you a drink and kissed you. How could I possibly get the wrong idea?' He kissed her again as "Start Me Up" from the Rolling Stones began to play.

As they kissed, one of the suits with an English accent got to the point.

'We're not staying. But everything's ready. You've got the go ahead. Tomorrow night at nine, sharp. You've got what you wanted. Your guns and ammo will be sailing into the port of Larne.'

'Don't mess it up,' another English suit said. 'The funds are in the account. Your contact is the UK's Russian Ambassador. He'll arrange for the arms drop. Royal Navy have been informed and won't intercept. Tomorrow, nine. Sharp.'

'Do you have many recruits?' one of the other suits asked.

'Five thousand at the moment,' Jonty's brother said. 'I'm meeting with the leader of the DUP tomorrow. They're going to stir things up at Stormont.'

'They'll need to do more than *stir things up*, they'll need to create a fucking disaster which we'll need to fix once the Deputy First and First Ministers step down, causing a collapse in government.'

'We've got it under control, don't you worry about that,' Jonty's brother said. 'We've even got a couple of lads paying a visit to Ballycastle tonight to light a few things up.'

'We'll be off then.' The suits made their way back out again, almost as if they couldn't wait to get away from the place.

Brendan hugged Lorna, kissing her neck, still hiding their faces as the suits left. The loyalists went upstairs for a game of snooker.

'Thought there was a CIRA meeting in here, not a loyalist meeting?' Lorna said.

'I know, what's Bobby playing at, is he trying to get me killed? Come on let's go.'

Leaving the club, they got back to the car and left the city, returning to Bobby's house. As he drove, Brendan wiped lipstick from his lips and fought to hide the smile from his face.

'Don't be getting carried away, you!' Lorna mumbled, biting her lip. Clearly, she wanted to remain professional. 'It was a necessity to get the job done today!'

'Of course it was,' Brendan said sarcastically. 'What do you fancy for dinner?'

'Whatever Bobby has in the house will do fine!'

'I'll make us some Spaghetti Bolognese.' Brendan fiddled with the radio until he arrived at Cool FM. There was a news report about a spate of attacks across Northern Ireland. Attacks on Catholic Gaelic Athletic clubs. A few chapels had been set on fire. They both knew that was the start of it. And they knew what was coming next. Undoubtedly it was going to be attacks on Protestant places of worship and eventually a few killings of some influential people, probably local leaders or even MLAs. That would be enough to antagonise the hard-line extremists on both sides. 'Fancy a drive up to Ballycastle tonight?'

'It'll be good to catch them in the act of whatever they're doing,' Lorna said. 'Our second piece of evidence.'

'Second?'

She played a recording of the meeting that took place in Frames.

'You're something else.' Brendan was impressed.

# Chapter Eight

AFTER A FORTY-MINUTE drive along the breath-taking Antrim coast, they approached the coastal village of Ballycastle. Looking across the water of the coastline three miles out, the village was only identifiable by the orange dots from the streetlights, dotted everywhere in a messy correlation.

As they got closer, Lorna pointed towards a building set out in the middle of nowhere, no other buildings around. 'What's that in the distance?' The building was ablaze.

'That's St Colm's chapel,' Brendan said. Lorna turned off the coastal road and went straight for the church.

On approach, they looked at the car parked on the grass verge just fifty meters away. They skidded to a halt, Brendan told Lorna to stay in the car.

'No chance,' she said, pulling her pistol out, checking the magazine. 'We're in this together.'

He threw the door open. 'Let's go and see if someone's...' he trailed off as he heard voices coming from the side of the building. As the voices got louder, he ducked behind a three-foot-high stone wall that surrounded the chapel grounds. Lorna got behind the car. Brendan watched as two men dressed in all black clothing and balaclavas ran past him. Squatting down in the shadows of the wall, he pulled his pistol out and shot them both in the feet. Their screams eventually went quiet as he approached them, his gun pointed directly at them.

'Shut your mouths, or I'll shut you both up permanently.'

Lorna approached, her gun also pointed at them. 'Who are you working for?' She kicked one of them as if the kick would cause an answer to fall out of their mouths.

'Fuck you, English bitch!' the larger of the two shouted.

She stepped on the foot that Brendan had just put a bullet in. 'Say that again?'

He screamed.

'I'm the nice one out of us two,' Brendan said. 'Now answer her question or you'll feel a lot more.' He pulled off their balaclavas. The one who'd kindly told Lorna to do one, had a shaven head, thin face and pointy nose. He had a Rangers tattoo below his left eye. Brendan poked the tattoo. 'Shouldn't that be "The Rangers" now?'

'Fuck you, taig!' He spat in Brendan's face.

Brendan stood up and wiped his face with his sleeve. Stepping again on the guys wounded foot. 'I'm half catholic and half protestant, I don't take sides.'

'I'll find out who you are, and you'll be shot!'

'I'm Brendan Cleary, and you can tell whoever sent you to do this, that I'm coming to get the rest of them.'

'So, you're the guy that killed Jonty?'

'What do you mean?'

'He died earlier today,' the guy with the Rangers tattoo sniggered. 'You're dead, mate. The UDA's going to do to you what they should have done to your da,' he laughed. 'You'll be shot before...'

Lorna put a bullet in his other foot. 'A fat man who looks like he lives off pints of Magners and kebabs would do well to keep his mouth shut. While he can still talk.'

'Back in a second.' Brendan turned and ran towards the car.

'Where are you going?' Lorna shouted.

Brendan ignored the question and ran straight for the boot. Finding some towing rope, he returned and threw it at the two, looking at the church as the building blazed on.

'Both of you roll over, onto your front.'

'Piss off, Cleary. Shoot us then.' The one with the tattoo shouted, then looked at Lorna. 'And you too, Brit!'

'Is he for real?' Lorna was astounded. Their stupidity was impressively bad. She put the pistol between his legs.

'Told you I was the nice one.' Brendan crouched down, forcing them to roll over, then searched their pockets, taking their phones and keys.

'Ian just keep your mouth shut,' the quieter of the two complained, almost crying. He was thin built, with shoulder length scruffy hair that clung to his sweat soaked face. 'Learn to just fucking shut it!' In contrast to the other, he didn't resist. Brendan tied them up. Listening to them groan in pain, Brendan looked at Lorna. 'At least they'll go down for arson.' He looked at the chapel that was now fully ablaze. Red and orange flames reaching far into the night sky above the roof.

'It's beyond saving now. The fire brigade couldn't even extinguish that,' Lorna said. 'We need to get moving. We can't be here.'

'Before we go,' Brendan kicked the one who was cooperating. 'What's the passcode to your phone.'

'1690'

Brendan sniggered. 'I should have known.'

They both ran back to the Audi. Brendan had a brainwave. 'I'll take their car. They may have something useful in it.'

He jumped into their vehicle – a dark Ford Mondeo. Both cars sped off in the direction they came from. Knowing the roads well, Brendan led the way, turning off the coastal road and heading in the direction of Ballymena.

They stopped at a petrol station. Filling both cars using Bobby's hard-earned drug money, they both made their way back towards his house.

Thirty minutes later after breaking the speed limit on the quieter roads, they pulled into the driveway, through the electric wooden gates and up towards the house. The rumbling of the tyres over the stones, broke what would have been complete night stillness in the countryside.

Pulling around the back of the house, they parked outside the garage. Brendan jumped out of the Ford and began searching for anything that could come in handy. He found a bag of guns stuffed into the spare wheel compartment, replacing the emergency breakdown kit. Closing the boot, the phone began to ring. Lorna reached into his pocket and pulled it out. The ringing stopped just as she was about to answer it.

'Shit. We could have had a nice chat to our friend who was in Frames today.' She put it in her pocket as they headed towards the house.

They walked into the kitchen. The lights came on automatically, then the phone beeped. A text message from the same number.

'The boss man must be doing the rounds with the calls, checking to see if they've all done what they've been instructed.'

'Okay. Respond to the text, saying that you've finished the job, successfully. You don't want to talk over the phone in case someone's listening in over the waves. Ask for confirmation about tomorrow and if there's anything else you can do.'

'1690,' she said, as she thumbed the passcode in then sent the text. 'I'm making a cup of tea, you want one?'

'Yeah, and some cheese and toast wouldn't go a miss either. I'm starving.'

Once they'd made the tea, and something to eat, they both dropped down onto Bobby's black leather sofa and tried to watch some mind-numbing television.

The rest of the night was spent commenting on all the poor and over the top acting. Without even realising the time passing by, they woke up after falling asleep beside each other, shocked awake by the vibrating of the loyalist's phone. The message read: *Be at the Larne harbour tomorrow at a quarter to nine. We need everyone fully operational tomorrow. Pick up your van to transport the guns. Vans are all waiting at the North-side Industrial Estate, Ballymena. Don't be late. We only get one chance at this.*

# Chapter Nine

AT SEVEN THIRTY, BRENDAN woke up, surprised to find Lorna had joined him in the bed. He rotated his head, trying not to wake her as she'd cuddled up to him. He could feel her breath on his neck. Taking his best shot, he moved in and gently kissed her on the lips. With her eyes still closed, she kissed him back running the palm of her hand affectionately down his cheek. The kiss grew with intensity as every second passed. Then her eyes shot open and jerked back, clearly confused about how she'd gotten there. 'What the hell?'

Sounding equally groggy, Brendan joked. 'Why don't you just admit it, you find me irresistible.' He reached in for another kiss, but this time she turned her face away and rolled him over onto his side of the bed. He laughed. 'You got into bed with me, not the other way around.'

'I must have been sleep walking!' She got out of the bed, revealing her long, toned legs and small shapely back, wearing nothing but black underwear. She walked over to the sliding wardrobe that ran all the way along the fifteen-foot wall, grabbed a robe for herself and tossed one on the bed. 'Wake your horny ass up. I'll go and make us breakfast.' She opened the door, shouting back to him as she walked down the hallway. 'Today is going to be a long day.'

'Say that again.' He mumbled as he lay there for a moment, just staring at the ceiling.

In the kitchen, neither of them mentioned the day ahead. Lorna was happy to work in silence, preparing them an Irish breakfast: sausages, bacon, eggs, potato bread and soda bread. All fried in the pan. A silver tray with a matching teapot sat brewing on the table. Bringing the food over to the table, she hummed, setting a plate on her side of the table, then handing Brendan his.

'Can't start the day without one of these,' Brendan said. 'My Nana Cleary used to make these all the time. I'd be full of energy for the rest of the day.' He jumped up from the stool. Grabbing the remote control, he turned on the thirty-inch plasma that was mounted on the wall at the corner, next to the patio doors that led into the football field-sized garden.

'Let's see what's happening in the world today!' He joked, planting himself back down on the stool.

'I think we've got a better idea about local affairs than the people watching the news,' Lorna said, her eyes fixed on the TV.

Brendan served the tea.

According to the news, British Prime Minster Nigel Thorn was talking about how he wanted to make a real change during his time in office. He said how he'd like to continue to focus on further developing the peace process in Northern Ireland.

'I'm sure you are,' Brendan mumbled, dipping his toast into the orange egg yolk. 'Is this whole mess as far up the chain as the prime minister?'

'Yes, but it'll be hard to link him to it, unless we can find evidence on him, or an associate.'

'If we can get ourselves a van full of weapons and take the one who's driving it, then we can squeeze as much information out of them as possible.' Brendan looked at his phone. Scrolling down through his Facebook news feed, he noticed his profile was awash with mentions. People were telling him he wouldn't be breathing much longer. Then he spotted something else. 'What the...' He handed the device to Lorna. Someone had posted a link to a story from the local news. The UTV news report said that Brendan was wanted on suspicion of murder, linked to the body in a burnt-out vehicle at Antrim's Newpark Industrial Estate. There were eyewitnesses that could testify to seeing him in the area. The report went on to claim how he'd apparently lost his mind because of the death of his grandfather who'd been buried the day before. He blamed British MI5 for the lifelong problems his father and grandfather had suffered. He looked at Lorna. 'Well, this just got a bit more serious. There's a manhunt for me now.'

She was reading the report but looked up, shaking her head in disbelief. 'The PSNI will be able to testify that...' she trailed off, realising what she was saying. 'There'll be a cover up - to say you were never lifted.'

'That'll clear me for Jonty's murder, then.' He sounded confused.

'But the murder of an M15 agent means they'll have agents hunting you down. Nobody gives a shit about some loyalist scumbag who died in a fight. But, an MI5 agent? That's a different story. They'll come at us with everything they've got.' She got up and went to the patio door. Lighting up a cigarette, she shook her head.

Brendan followed her. Taking it off her, he said, 'thought you were giving it up?'

'I'll give them up when this is over.' She took it back off him and took a long draw of it, exhaling it as if her problems were drifting into the air with the smoke.

Brendan looked down the garden as the rain began to pelt down. 'Fuck it, I'm going down to Milltown Cemetery. Best place in the world for clearing my head.'

'Brendan, your grandfather was only buried two days ago. They'll have people watching the place.'

'If they're watching it, I'll give them a nice surprise. You can come or you can stay here until I get back, it's up to you!'

She took another drag from her cigarette and threw it to the ground, continuing to shake her head. 'Shit, Brendan.' She looked at him, her eyes piercing.

'I'm not going to roll over and hide from them.'

'Right, let's go. I've got an idea who might be on surveillance detail. A little weasel called Matthew Hilton. He had his nose so far up Hughes' ass that I wouldn't be surprised that it was him that set us up to be shot.'

'I'll look forward to getting my hands on him.'

# Chapter Ten

CRUISING DOWN THE CRUMLIN Road part of North Belfast – a dividing carriageway that acted as a single stretch that separated the IRA dominated Cliftonville Road and the UDA controlled Shankill Road – Brendan and Lorna both sat quietly, their unease evident to the other. Perhaps it was because they were both somehow caught up in Belfast's potential return to civil unrest. An unthinkable, somewhat laughable thought that would leave a normal Belfast resident laughing. But, no matter how much either of them would fight to prove it wasn't true, the facts were: Brendan was now wanted for murdering a commanding M15 agent, and that same agent had their brains splat all over the car shared with both Brendan and Lorna. It didn't take a genius to figure out something dodgy was going on. And at a high level in government.

As they reached the end of Crumlin Road, merging onto the Carlisle Circus roundabout, both glanced at the area where Hughes had met his end.

'Don't know whether to be sad or happy,' Lorna said, as she put the window down. 'Sad about Hughes or happy that we didn't join him.'

'Maybe not happy, but grateful. We've an opportunity to finish whoever shot him, before they come back for a second shot.' Brendan reached under his seat, pulling out a black backpack. Checking it had the guns in it, he looked at Lorna who was guiding the Audi onto the Westlink, taking them over to the west of the city towards the cemetery.

It was shortly after one o'clock and the usual lunch time rush had plagued the roads like a swarm of locusts. And after a few near misses with other road users, they finally reached the cemetery.

'Maybe it's better to park on the street and walk in,' Lorna said, 'it's a good thing it's pouring down. We can throw our hoods up without looking suspicious.'

'Aye,' Brendan said. 'Let's go. I think there's an umbrella in the boot if you want it.'

Lorna pulled the car over into a roadside parking bay and paid the one-pound fee for the hour. They both linked arms, under the umbrella with their hoods up.

As they entered the grounds, they realised they were the only people there, not surprising given the weather.

'Don't know if it's a good thing or a bad thing being the only people in here.'

'Looks like we're not!' Lorna hissed, simultaneously tightening her grip around Brendan's arm.

He looked up and seen a grey Jaguar XE. Two front seat occupants could just about be seen through the window's reflection.

'What does this "weasel" look like?' Brendan asked. 'If that's him, we might need to go and say hello.'

'Let's walk on up past the car, I need to get a better look.' They both quickened their pace. 'Don't look at any grave that belongs to your family, that'll be a dead giveaway.'

With heads down, linked closely together, they got within fifty yards of the Jag. 'That's him, Brendan. The backstabbing bastard!' Lorna gripped Brendan's arm hard, almost cutting the circulation. 'Let's walk past. See how on edge he is. Anxiety is the best indicator someone's done wrong and they know it.'

They had to walk directly past the car to stay on the footpath. Had they walked on the muddy grass just to keep a distance from the car, they would have looked too suspicious. Twenty feet from the car, Lorna unlinked her arm from Brendan's. Pulling her pistol out of her handbag, she marched straight for the driver's window, gun pointed straight at the car. She fired one shot. The window shattered, followed by a yell. She hadn't killed the target.

Jumping into auto-pilot mode, Brendan produced his pistol and ran around to the passenger side. Pointing it directly at the seat's occupant. Opening the door, he grabbed a heavy-set middle-aged male out by the tie, shock written all over the man's face. The man fell, his grey trousers instantly caked in mud; crouching down as if in silent prayer, facing the ground, afraid to look at Brendan.

'Get him back in the car,' Lorna hissed.

Brendan grabbed him again by the tie, pulling him back to his feet, bowling him back into his seat. Lorna had the driver with his hands cable-tied to the steering wheel.

'Get in the back, Brendan.' She jumped into the back behind the driver. Brendan did the same on the opposite side.

'Thanks for tinting your windows,' Brendan said, breathing heavily. 'Now what are you pair doing sitting here watching my grandfather's grave?'

'We were waiting for you pair to turn up, and it looks like we were right.' The man in the passenger seat forced a laugh, trying to sound confident, but his sporadically jumping vocal chords said otherwise. He wrestled with his tie, loosening it from his neck.

'Don't know why you're both sounding so chuffed with yourselves,' Lorna said, 'given the fact you've guns pointed at your heads. Now, what are you all planning, and why did you kill Hughes - and try to kill us?'

'That's classified,' the driver groaned, struggling for a breath from behind the steering wheel. 'Come on, Lorna. You've been through enough training. You know we can't give you that information.' He sniggered. 'Sorry.'

'You should stop with the jokes, Matt.' She forced her pistol into the back of his head. 'I'm not afraid to use this. But that would be too easy. Brendan here will torture you so much that you'll be begging him to just kill you.' She looked at Brendan. 'Brendan Cleary – meet agent Matthew Hilton. Matt, meet Brendan Cleary.'

'It's a pleasure.' Brendan spoke sarcastically. 'Why'd you set me up for Hughes' murder? And what have you just dragged me into?'

'Fuck you, Cleary!' The agent in the passenger seat said.

Brendan reached around the seat in front of him and grabbed the agent by the ear, twisting it so hard that he thought for a second it had stretched. 'My father used to do this when I stepped out of line, and I tell you what, it made sure I didn't do whatever it was again.'

'Is that all he taught you?' The agent laughed as Brendan let go. 'Very sophisticated.'

'Brendan, meet Malcolm Rogers. He's always been a dip shit, even during his recruitment training.' Lorna sighed through her words.

'How's your mother?' Hilton looked at Brendan in the rear-view mirror.

'She's dead,' Brendan said. 'Drank herself to death. But of course, you knew that.'

Lorna cleared her throat. A silence fell over the cabin.

Brendan cleared his throat, then pulled a knife out of his pocket. He reached over to the driver's seat, and with his knife, grabbed Hilton's index finger, cutting the tip off. A red dotted line of blood splattered along the windscreen. Hilton's screams almost shattered the car's windows. Brendan pressed in the cigarette lighter and waited for it to pop. Pulling it out of the housing, he looked at the red glow, almost in admiration for the pain it was about to deliver. Pressing the hot end on top of the severed fingertip, the sizzling of cooked flesh, caused both Lorna and the other agent to wince. Hilton's screams were terrifying, his entire body went into aggressive spasms, the cable ties cutting into his wrists, drawing blood.

Sitting back in his seat as Hilton sobbed, Brendan wiped the blood on the side of the seat. Rogers screamed for help.

'If you don't want the same as him, shut your mouth,' Brendan said.

'What do you want to know?' Hilton cried. 'I'll tell you anything, just don't hurt me, again. Please, please don't hurt me again!'

'Who ordered Hughes and me to be shot?' Lorna said, as she videoed the scene with her phone.

'It goes way to the top.'

'Who, you piece of shit,' Lorna shouted, forcing her pistol into the side of Hilton's head. 'Before Brendan takes another digit!'

'Robert Smith brought his annual report to the home secretary and the prime minister with recommendations to take you out!' Hilton said.

Brendan looked at Lorna. 'Who's this Smith?'

'Director General for MI5,' she said. 'And you? You fed the info to Smith?'

'No!' Hilton protested, 'it wasn't me, I swear!'

'Listen to him crying like a fucking baby!' Brendan said. 'Did you think about Hughes when you set him up to be slaughtered? Did MI5 give a shit about my family?' He jumped up from his seat and took the tip off Hilton's middle finger.

'That's enough, Brendan!' Lorna said. 'We'll let the authorities deal with them, you don't want to incriminate yourself any more on video. We've got what we need!'

'What are you going to do with us?' Rogers said, a hint of hope in his voice that they would be spared. 'I have a wife and a...'

'What about what my family, you piece of shit!' Brendan jumped up and busted Rodgers on the side of the head with the handle of his gun.

'Brendan!' Lorna shouted this time, dragging him back down onto the seat. 'We've got what we need from them.'

'Not quite,' Brendan said. 'As much as the thought turns my stomach, we should become these two clowns to get closer to Smith. He's the one I'm going after next.'

'The higher we go, the harder it's going to get,' Lorna said. 'I hope you're ready for this to get much messier.' She took out another pistol from her handbag. Pointing it first at Rogers, listening to him scream, she shot him in the neck with a tranquilliser dart. Following with the same into Hilton's neck. 'You drive this one and I'll take your uncle's Audi back to his house.'

'Fair enough,' Brendan said. 'He can go in the boot!' He gestured towards Hilton who was out cold with his head back against the headrest.

'Just drag him into the back for now, we don't know who's watching us. Smith could have people watching these two fools. Clearly they're incompetent and Smith's smart; he'd know this pair would need help.'

'Let's hope you're wrong.' Brendan jumped up from his seat, dragging Hilton's dead weight into the back, ripping every button off his shirt in the process. 'I've never been so grateful to have tinted windows before,' he said, climbing into the driver's seat beside a sleeping Rogers. 'Right, stay behind me.' He started the engine as Lorna got out.

# Chapter Eleven

ARRIVING BACK AT BOBBY'S house, now in possession of a government issue vehicle, Brendan parked it in the garage, leaving Bobby's Mitsubishi in the driveway.

Lorna pulled up behind the Japanese rally car. 'Your uncle owns some nice cars.'

'All bought with drug and racketeering money,' Brendan mumbled. 'And he's only my uncle by marriage, not a blood relative.' For the second time since they'd met, he'd felt the need to make that clear.

'What's for dinner?' Lorna asked, shrugging at Brendan's statement.

'Let's go have a look, I'm starving.'

As they entered the kitchen, Lorna stopped, gasping in shock. The cupboards were open, drawers pulled out and the contents scattered all over floor.

Brendan signalled to Lorna, his finger across his lips. Her gaze pierced him as she pulled her pistol out, gesturing for him to do the same. Just as he did so, a thud came from the ceiling above them.

'They're still here,' he whispered, stepping slowly towards the door that led to the hallway. He gripped his pistol and slowly opened the door, drawing in mumbles from the stairway. There were at least two. 'We'll wait for them to come down,' he whispered, closing the door again.

'But where's their car?' Lorna hissed. 'There's nothing in the driveway.'

'Good question.' Brendan kept his eyes on the ceiling, the movements sounding as if they were dragging a dead body.

'If they're clever enough to think about us coming back, and left no outside sign of forced entry, then we're dealing with professionals!' Lorna said.

The footsteps above moved faster, with more thud, sending vibrations tingling down through the six light cluster pendant light, dangling in the centre of the ceiling. The sound of a door closing was next. The footsteps moved further away, until they started thumping down the stairs.

Brendan double checked his pistol was loaded.

'Nervous? Tough guy?' Lorna joked. The claps of shoes across the marble floor got louder. They were right outside the door. As the door handle lowered, Lorna pulled it open, then instantly slammed it closed again. She pulled the door open again and found two men on the ground, both wearing balaclavas, dressed in black woollen jumpers, stonewash jeans and sandy coloured boots. The one in the front who was floored by the door was dragged upright by their partner. Lorna and Brendan both pointed their guns at them.

'Take your masks off!' Brendan said. 'Drop your gun,' he said to the one that was helping other up.

They set their guns down, raising their hands, slowly backing away. 'Don't shoot, just...take it easy.' An Englishman's voice sounded genuinely worried behind the mask.

'You're English?' Lorna sounded confused. 'Englishmen have joined the paramilitaries again.'

'They've always been involved,' Brendan joked. 'Did you find what you were looking for?'

'I'll go check the place out, you watch this pair.' Lorna headed for the stairs.

After ordering the two of them into the kitchen and closing the door, Brendan sat on the ground with his back against the door. 'So,' he said, ready to make small talk to break the silence, 'what's the craic? Who sent you? You're here looking for me or Bobby?'

'It's a good thing you ask,' the Englishman said. 'Your uncle told us you were here!' He laughed. 'Your own family ratted on you!'

'He's not my family,' Brendan protested. 'If it weren't for my aunt, he wouldn't have been anything more than another wannabe hard man wanting to be linked to the Cleary name.'

'Yes, that's right. Damien was quite the legend around here, wasn't he?' he replied sarcastically.

Brendan shot him in the foot. 'The government have definitely sent the best, then.' He stood up as the man screamed, gripping his foot. 'Dry your eyes, you'll live. In fact, both of you get up. And go over there, towards the dining room.'

The wounded was assisted by the other to get across the room, bloody footprints left behind with every step. Both sat at the table. Brendan pulled a sandwich bag full of cable ties out and ordered the non-wounded one to cable tie the other's feet and hands together. Brendan set the gun down on the twelve-seat mahogany table. Snatching the cable ties up from the table, he ordered the unbound one to put his hands out. As Brendan cable tied his hands and feet together, he heard footsteps coming from the room upstairs. He waited for a few minutes while watching the two. Neither of them said a word.

After a few minutes with no sign of Lorna, Brendan made his way towards the mansion's spiralling staircase. He wasn't sure what was waiting for him up there. One thing he was sure of – it was too quiet. He tip-toed up the flight of thirty stairs, his pistol ready. He knew there was a good chance he'd have to use it. But he was programmed to kill, without hesitation or remorse, thanks to his father, so if it were needed, he'd have no problem. Did he always have the same mentality as the late Damien Cleary or was it only during the training that he was moulded into the man his father wanted him to be? He wasn't sure. What he was sure about was, he wasn't hesitant about any of it. He seemed to be taking it all in his stride.

He got to the top of the stairs. The white carpet lined first floor made it easy for his approach to go unheard, and the fact the house was modern helped, too – no creaky floorboards to give him away. His only issue was all five of the bedroom doors were closed and he'd no idea which one to try first. He *was* walking into the line of fire. Lorna was in one of those rooms and she'd need him to come and help her. Where else was she? It didn't make sense for her just to disappear and go silent like she had. There *was* a third intruder.

Arriving at the first door, he stopped, listening closely. He couldn't hear a thing. He continued onto the second. Still nothing. Then he tried the door facing the one he was at. Nothing again, until he stepped away and heard water running from the inside. Whatever it was, Lorna hadn't just decided to freshen up. But he was undecided what to do.

He thought for a moment. His eyes darting everywhere, trying to piece a plan of action together. Then came a man's voice.

'Lorna, drop to the fucking ground, now!'

'Brendan, aim high!' She responded.

Brendan put three bullets through the door at head height, then shot out the lower and upper hinges. Kicking the door in, he jumped back behind the wall. Then came gunfire. Three shots.

'He has a Desert Eagle!' Lorna shouted. '.5 0.'

'Shut up, you bitch!' An English voice shouted.

Lorna screamed.

Brendan took his phone out and put the camera on selfie mode. He craned his right arm out into the firing line and took a photo. Another two shots rang out. So that was five shots the gun had fired. And since a .5 0 Desert Eagle only had seven rounds in the magazine, he knew there were only two shots left. Brendan had used five bullets from his Glock. But he didn't want to fire any unnecessary shots into a room where Lorna was.

He needed their gun to run out of ammo so he could go in there and take him down with his hands. That, he was confident he could do. He reached his arm around the doorway again and purposefully shot into the air, knowing Lorna was on the ground, the gun in the room responded with another two shots. Before the gun could be reloaded, he dropped his pistol and lunged from behind the wall.

Seeing the size of the masked man he knew his hands were going to be full. Lorna was on the ground at the guy's feet.

'I've toyed with guys twice your size,' the giant laughed. 'Come on, then, you little Irish rodent!' He launched his Dessert Eagle at Brendan.

Brendan shielded his face, the pistol bouncing off his forearm, sending the nerves rattling up his funny bone. His adrenaline masked the pain. The opponent was an imposing six and a half foot tall, at least, with shoulders wider than the doorway. He easily towered over Brendan.

He swung for Brendan, but Brendan blocked the blow, and side kicked his shin. He flinched but didn't go down; instead rugby tackling Brendan into the wardrobe. A laundry basket full of clothes came down on top of them. It was now a rumble on the ground. The man's heavier body was pinning Brendan to the ground. He punched Brendan in the gut, winding him. Brendan did the only thing he could do in that moment with the man continuing to throw blows into his stomach, he latched onto the man, wrapping his legs around his waist and clinging onto him. With his hands he pulled his balaclava off and bit into the man's ear, tearing the top corner of it off. The man screamed. Brendan spat the piece of ear at the man and plugged his two thumbs into his eyes. He rolled off Brendan, screaming, frantically massaging his eyes.

Brendan sprang to his feet, looking at Lorna who was staring at him with wide eyes. 'What?' Brendan said. He crouched down, grabbed the man by the head and plunged it into the wall, knocking him unconscious. He ran over to Lorna. She was tied up with suit ties. He sniggered. 'Very sophisticated.'

He cut her free, then tied the intruder up. Lorna watched him while Brendan ran back down the stairs. The other two were gone.

'Fuck,' he shouted, running to the sink. He rinsed his mouth out then cleaned the cut on his knuckle. Reaching into the cupboard below the sink, he pulled out a first aid kit. He snatched an antiseptic wipe and cleaned the cut. Running to the downstairs bathroom, he took some mouth wash. Feeling fresher, he ran upstairs to find Lorna having a discussion with the giant as he pressed a towel to his ear while another towel soaked up the blood gushing from his mouth.

'He's been quite the talker, our new friend here!' Lorna said, standing up, caressing her bruised wrists. 'He was sent by your Uncle Bobby.'

'He's not my fucking uncle,' Brendan shouted. 'And I'll deal with him myself when we find him.'

'What about your aunt, his wife?'

'She can handle herself,' Brendan said, walking over to the wounded. 'Where can we find the one who put you up to this? And not Bobby.'

Before he could reply, Lorna interrupted. 'It's all coming from the top, Brendan. There's no point in going after anyone else. It's a waste of time. We know who we've got to get. We know where to find them.' She dragged him outside the room to talk privately. 'We go to the arms drop tonight. We get some more evidence. Then we go straight for Smith. We'll find him hiding behind his desk in London. But when we go there, we'll only have one chance so it's got to be planned right.'

'Right, well let's go now. The other pair downstairs have got away...'

'Shit!' Lorna said.

'We'll not be back here again, so let's go. Now!'

They grabbed their stuff. Grateful to have Bobby's bank card, they left.

'I guess we'll need a new car.' Lorna dove into the passenger seat of the Audi.

Brendan jumped into the driver's seat. 'Actually, if we're going to play the role of Hilton and Rogers, let's take their car. We'll leave them in the garage.

# Chapter Twelve

ON THE WAY TOWARDS the M2 motorway, northbound for the seaport town of Larne, Brendan looked at Lorna, his expression less serious, more of inappropriate amusement, given their situation.

'What's that charming little grin for, Brendan Cleary?'

He broke into a child-like, innocent grin. 'You look really sexy sitting there. Tight fitting black clothes. Like an olden day cat burglar.'

'What do you want to me the wear? A high-vis shell suit?' She said. 'Very discreet. And look at you – Mr Hardman, just out of the gym with your tracksuit bottoms and hoodie. You look like a glue-sniffing joy-rider.'

'I could have been one of those,' he mumbled. 'All my mates were, but my father would have kicked my ass!'

'He did you a favour, then,' Lorna said. 'Where are all your joyriding, glue-sniffing mates now?'

'A couple are dead. Some were kneecapped by the IRA and some were told to leave the country or be shot!'

'So be grateful for him threatening to kick your ass to keep you in line. He did it for your own good.'

'Maybe. Fancy a coffee? I need to get petrol anyway.' Brendan gestured at the approaching fuel station, "Go" plastered everywhere in bold red writing.

'I'll have a cup of tea.'

'Think I might, too.' He guided the vehicle into pump eight and switched off the ignition. He grabbed his phone and jumped out. While gunning in fifty quid worth of unleaded into the TFSI Quattro, he suspiciously watched every person in the vicinity. He was not only on the run, but also had a government target on his back. He looked into the car, barely able to see Lorna's dark outline through the darkened windows, realising it truly was them against the world. A lady who'd looked at him on the floor of a jail cell only days prior as if he was some street hood. Now they were thrust into a race against time to not only save their own lives but prevent the potential return of paramilitary violence throughout the still unstable six counties of Northern Ireland.

Walking into the petrol station, Brendan quickly regretted the idea of coming in for a cup of tea. The newspaper stall publicised not only his, but Lorna's mug shot on the front.

'Shit.' He put his head down and chose to use the self-service. After quickly grabbing two drinks, he left and paid the fuel by card at the pump.

Jumping into the car, he handed Lorna – who was glaring at her phone – her tea. 'Guess what?'

'I know.' She sighed. 'I knew it wouldn't be long before I'd become wanted, too. Thank *God* you didn't bring me out tea as white as a sheet. I hate when people do that.' Clearly unfazed by the fact she was now being hunted down, she took a sip of tea. 'Not bad. Let's go.'

After purchasing a P&O ticket, they were granted access. Passing through the port's security, they joined the queue of travellers, waiting on the ferry. Brendan shut the engine off, beside a portable waiting area where there were comfortable sofas and refreshments available for purchase. The clock said eight twenty-two. Forty minutes early for the drop. He watched a fleet of six black Renault Sprinters arrive.

Hilton's mobile vibrated in Brendan's pocket. It was a text. It read: *Royal Navy has let the Russian fishing trawler named "The Russian Trident" make it's way towards the port. It's due to arrive shortly after nine. We have people waiting outside the homes of the first and deputy first ministers.*

Brendan looked at Lorna. 'Jesus Christ, there's going to be a blood bath.' He handed her the phone. 'They plan on taking out the ministers.'

'God, Brendan!' she said, 'they're going to start taking people out tonight. Not next week, or in two months – tonight.' She handed him back the phone. 'We can't afford to let any of the ministers get killed. The ministers on both sides have been directly involved in the conflict, leading the paramilitaries. They have a lot of old-time followers, comrades that will not be happy if they were to be assassinated.'

A black Mercedes drove past them, heading towards the vans. They watched as the drivers of the six Sprinters got out. A well-dressed suit who looked like a bodyguard emerged from the driver's seat. He walked to the back of the car and opened the door, allowing a tubby, middle-aged man step out. He looked around the area, as if expecting he'd been followed, then walked towards the group of van drivers, one of which sparked Brendan and Lorna's intrigue. Mervyn Coulter.

'Shit, that's my uncle – what's he doing here?'

'Mervyn Coulter is related to you?' Lorna said. 'Shit,' she paused, looking at him, 'he is, isn't he? He was one of the reasons MI5 recruited your father all those years back.' She gestured to the frail old man, wrapped in a Linfield football scarf and matching woollen hat. 'That bastard was responsible for the loss of many lives.'

'He was the sworn enemy of my father's side during the seventies. The only thing they ever agreed on was that Lenny Murphy needed putting to sleep.' Brendan laughed sarcastically. 'So Mervyn here, gave Murphy up to my father's brothers.'

'I'm sure the IRA loved getting their hands on that twisted bastard. He created a new wave of terror, never seen before in this part of the world.' She looked at Brendan, then through the windscreen again, gesturing towards his uncle. 'But it's a surprise he's here. He hasn't been seen for years. He stepped away from the whole scene once the 1994 ceasefire came into effect.'

'He was a bitter old bastard according to my grandfather Cleary and it doesn't surprise me that if there's going to be another – even fabricated – return to violence, he's going to be involved in it. He'll probably want one more stab at the Irish Catholic culture before his time's up.'

Lorna looked at Brendan. 'So, you're not a big fan of this one then?'

'I'll have no problem putting a bullet in him if I have to.'

They continued to watch Brendan's uncle act like the loyalist's advisor to the suit. The suit accompanied Mervyn on a walk-around tour of the vans, revealing empty spaces. Soon to be filled.

Three marked police cars arrived. Yet none of the van drivers appeared concerned about their arrival. Instead, they were greeted by smiles and handshakes as they joined the party.

Taking on the role of a photographer, Brendan took out his Galaxy and began taking photos of the crowd. He'd taken about thirty when Lorna stopped him.

'You need to email them to yourself in case something happens to your phone.' She looked at the group, all returning to their vehicles, perhaps getting ready to load up. 'I've set up a private email address which M15 don't know about. You can send all the evidence to that. Set yourself up a private email address and we can both have copies.'

After setting up a private account, Brendan done what she advised. 'There'll be many more of those to come,' he said, as the police cars drove past, not even giving them a second glance. 'It's a good thing we chose this car. These dumbasses think we're Hilton and Rogers.'

'We've got movement,' Lorna said, watching the six vans all reverse closer to the water as a forty-five-foot-long, bright white trawler glided along the edge of the port. From the distance it was hard to spot the name or number along the side, but the fishing vessel had the horizontal tricolour of white, blue and red: the Russian flag extending from the mast. 'That's them.' Lorna looked in her bag checking she had ammo. 'Okay, I've got an idea.'

'Go for it.'

'This car is proving useful, especially when people think we're on their side, but we can probably make use of having a police car to help keep the authorities off our backs!'

'If you can't beat them, join them.' Brendan said. He turned and looked at the port's entrance. One of the police cars remained. 'You want to join the PSNI?'

'Not really,' Lorna said, 'besides, you've probably had a lot more experience in those cars than I have.'

Brendan shook his head and started the engine. Driving towards the marked car, he pulled up alongside the driver's side. Just a few feet between him and an arresting officer, and nothing but a tinted window stopping the officer from realising who was behind the wheel. He checked his gun was loaded and the silencer fitted, then pulled his hood up over his head. Waiting for the cop to look in the opposite direction, he stepped out of the car, pointing his gun at the officer. The officer looked over, his eyes widened, jumping with fright. He froze on the spot as Brendan ran over, ordering him out of the car. As he stepped out, before he could even shout for help, Brendan flipped the gun around in his hand and clocked him on the temple, sending the officer to the ground. When he struggled to his feet holding his bleeding temple, Brendan thumped him a second time, this time knocking him out.

Brendan grabbed the unconscious officer's cuffs and took great pleasure in fitting them to his limp wrists. Opening the boot he measured with his eyes that there was enough room to bowl the officer in. There was. Brendan took off his hoodie and put on the officer's shirt and hat. The shirt size was XL. Brendan was a medium build. It made him look like a dwarf inside. He put on the black tie and hat, then used one of the officer's socks to gag him.

Taking control of the police issue weapon and communication, he got behind the wheel. He looked over at Lorna who was grinning at him.

'Congratulations on your new appointment, you look good in that suit,' she said, as she moved into the driver's seat of Hilton's vehicle. 'Very cute, Officer Cleary!'

'Piss off.' Brendan smirked. The radio's static changed. A voice came through.

'Our Russian friends have arrived. We need you to escort one of the vans to it's destination. Officer 8488, you will be escorting your van to Pennybridge Industrial Estate, Ballymena.'

Brendan looked at the badge on his shirt. Officer 8488. 'Roger that,' he said response to the command. He looked at Lorna, stalking the fleet. 'Do you know this Pennybridge Industrial Estate in Ballymena?'

'I know Ballymena. How hard can it be to find? I'll check the sat nav. Do you want me to go on ahead?'

'It's probably better. If they see two cars following them, they'll get nervous.'

'Okay, I'll get moving now.'

'Be careful!' Brendan said.

'Brendan, you sound concerned!' Lorna smirked, then blew him a kiss.

He just smiled back at her.

'Looks like you'll be right behind me anyway.' She gestured towards the vans. Two of them pulling away from the trawler. 'See you soon!'

# Chapter Thirteen

ON THE WAY DOWN THE A36, west bound from the Antrim coast towards Ballymena, Brendan received a call from Lorna.

'Brendan, we've got quite a few people down here at Penny-bridge. We need to be careful not to get spotted. If we get into a gun battle with this crowd, we're dead. We'll have no chance.'

'Okay,' Brendan said, lowering the window, letting some crisp sea air cool his face. 'Plan B, then!'

'Plan B?'

'We'll have to take the vehicle before it reaches Ballymena.'

'Risky, Brendan. But it might be worth it. How far away are you?'

'About ten minutes.'

'Okay, you pull the van over, along the side of the road. I'll double back and meet you.' Lorna paused. 'And, Brendan – be careful. There's no point being a bloody hero and getting killed.'

'Aw,' Brendan joked. 'I love you too, dear.'

'Just be careful, or I'll kick your ass when I get my hands on you. I don't want to have to go out my way to save your stupid ass.'

Brendan ended the call and activated the siren. The van started to slow, finally pulling over onto the side of the road.

Stepping out into the rain, marble sized raindrops pelting off the van provided some cover for Brendan. Keeping his head down, he ran alongside the van, approaching the driver's door just as the window went down.

'What's happening?' The man shouted out the window. He had chin length, scruffy hair; a round face with a boxer's nose. The *Fuck The Pope* tattoo on his forearm said he was likely someone who'd enjoy bringing some bloodshed to the Catholics of the land.

Brendan gave the man barely a moment to utter a word another word. He pointed his gun at him and ordered him to get out.

With his hands in the air, the driver stepped out. The rain had picked up, the whooshing sound of cars flying past at sixty mph reminded Brendan there were eyes everywhere. Eyes he couldn't afford to have on him.

'What's happening, Brendan Cleary?' the man shouted, sarcastically. 'Didn't know you'd joined the peelers. How's your grandfather?' He sniggered. He was about to continue when Brendan shot him in the neck.

As he pulled the van's side door open, a black sports bag fell out, hitting the ground with a clunk. A least he knew he wouldn't be running out of weapons anytime soon. He dumped the loyalist into the back of the van, on top of a stack of bags similar to the one that was lying at his feet.

He slammed the sliding door closed and got behind the wheel, calling Lorna.

'Brendan, is everything okay?'

'I'm behind the wheel of our friend's van. I'm going to put the weapons into the police car and leave the van here. The driver's taking a nap in the back.'

'Okay. Get off that road as quick as you can. There's a service station just before you reach Ballymena. Meet me there and we'll move the guns again.'

Flying up through the gears, Brendan took full advantage of the fact he could use the siren, leaving the speed limit behind with the empty van. Progressing along the road towards the station, he listened to the ten o'clock news report. The report talked about two men found dead at the scene of an arson attack on a chapel between Ballycastle and Carnlough. He was surprised to hear that the two men were dead, but he wasn't fazed. He knew there'd be an ever-growing body-count before it was all done, but it was better the body-count were people who chose to get involved in it, rather than innocent people. The report went on to repeat the claims of Brendan Cleary being a suspect in the murder of the undercover MI5 agent in Antrim Town and Brendan's accomplice was the London born agent Lorna Woodward.

As he approached the service station, he spotted headlights in the corner of the empty car park. Lorna flashing him over. He reversed into the bay beside her.

'The two arsonists are dead, according to the news,' she said, as she got out of the car.

'Heard it on the radio. Guess they got what they deserved.'

'A lot more will get the same.' Lorna looked at the car she'd taken from Hilton. 'And I won't lose any sleep over whoever has to die. Right, let's get these guns somewhere safe. Do you know anywhere people wouldn't check?'

'Well, we can't go back to Bobby's house. But I think I know somewhere we could use. It's in a little village between Belfast and Antrim. Templepatrick. It was my father's place of relaxation and getting away from it all, without having to travel all the way over to the west coast.'

'Let's go!'

Lorna got back into the government issue vehicle and waited for Brendan to take the lead. The time was ten fifteen and they were about to end the most insane day of their lives. A new wave of violence was looming, just around the corner; and the mayhem of the day would perhaps serve as a simple warm-up for what was coming. With five van loads of government-funded weapons in the hands of people hell-bent on bringing the bullets and bombs back to the streets of Belfast, the inevitable was either: innocent lives being lost, or a number of backward thinking thugs would perish, leaving their families to be the ones to pick up the pieces. That was the reality of it all. And somehow the two most unlikely couple were the two that could either stop it, or become another statistic in the long line of people to perish because of it.

After taking off, Brendan called Lorna and asked her to stay patched through on the call as they got closer to the house. 'I'm pretty sure people won't know about this place. But after today, I can't be certain about anything anymore.' He led the way past the village shopping mall and took the first left, leading them down a sloping estate of tree lined avenues. The large detached houses, armed with luxurious cars in the driveway were a clear indicator that Damien Cleary Jnr was a man who didn't need to worry much about his finances. Brendan pulled into the empty driveway of number 84, driving right up to the white double garage doors.

He stepped out into a garden that would have looked like a quality public park had it not been for the untreated grass and outlining hedges. He ran over to a group of rocks presented in the shape of a bird, decorated within a flowerbed. Picking up the rock which acted as one of the eyes, he pulled a set of keys from under it.

Lorna got out of her car. 'God, your father pulled that trick right out of an American 80s flick.' She looked at the car. 'Better get this car out of sight.'

'He always kept himself a few motors. He had one here, I think,' Brendan unlocked the garage and rolled the door up. There sat a car of class. An Audi A5, three litre Quattro. 'Like this three-door beast.'

'Nice,' Lorna said. 'I prefer this than the A8.'

Brendan jumped in behind the wheel of the luxurious German, momentarily admiring the cream leather interior and trim. He felt under the driver's seat. Slipping his fingers into a pocket that had been stitched to the seat's base, he pulled out the key, knowing that the car would not only start first time, but had a full tank of unleaded. His father was OCD when it came to preparation.

After swapping the vehicles around, they went into the house through the front door. Given the fact that the front garden was more like a secluded football field, lined with evergreens and a ten-foot high mahogany fence, there was no need to sneak in the back door.

As they stepped into the hallway, Brendan called lights and heating on. The command was honoured, the boiler could be heard firing up with a slight rumble. 'I love this place, it was always my sanctuary,' he said, walking along the hallway towards a set of double doors. Walking into the living room, he dropped a bag of guns onto the marble floor and stepped out of his shoes, heading towards the roaring fire that had just ignited. 'This was my favourite place as a kid. It's also where I came to study.'

'Brendan, you're losing your badboy image,' Lorna teased. 'You're telling me the guy I found lying on the floor of a cell with a hangover and a swollen face was a model student?'

'My father always made sure I understood that our ability to think was much more valuable than our ability to use our hands.'

'I can tell by the way you talk and the words you use you're not just some random thug off the streets.' Lorna took her shoes off and sat on the rug, pulling her knees up to her face as if fighting to contain heat. She looked directly into the flames as if looking for an answer.

Brendan sat down, mirroring her. 'I just buried the most important person in my life the other day. Since my father disappeared, Grandda became my best friend. I'm starting to think he knew more than others did, certainly more than he let on. Maybe he knew this was coming and wanted to prepare for it. I wonder how much he knew about my father, his son, and didn't tell me.' He looked up at the ceiling, wearing the same thoughtful expression Lorna had given to the fire. 'If he's watching over me, I'll make sure he's proud.' He stopped, feeling as if he had a ball in his throat, his eyes glazed over.

Lorna gripped his hand. 'Well let's make him proud.' She moved in to kiss him on the cheek, but he turned to look at her.

Their lips met. They kissed slowly, their lips barely touching, but enough to feel each other's. Brendan caressed her cheek, then ran his fingertips slowly up her face and through her hair as the kiss got more intense. They rolled back onto the rug, shadows from the flames dancing off them as the kiss continued.

The sound of a phone vibrating in one of the bags ended the moment. They separated.

'Bloody phones,' Lorna said, as she rolled over and got to her feet. 'Let's hope this is good news.' She hopped up off the ground, staggering over to the bag. Rustling through it, she pulled out a Nokia. 'It's the brigadier.' She looked at Brendan. 'Probably checking in on the drivers.'

'Well, *you* can't answer it,' Brendan said, reaching for the phone. 'Give it to me.' He took the phone and before he had a chance to answer, the call ended. Brendan waited for a retry, but a text came through instead.

*Keep your eyes peeled tonight, don't be getting caught. If you do, keep your traps shut or it'll get us all into shit! Be ready for a lot of eyes on Stormont tomorrow.*

Brendan looked at the bag, as if trying to work out a riddle. 'Someone's going to be shot at Stormont tomorrow, or worse, blown up.'

'With the police involved, they have everything they need to do it and not get caught,' Lorna said. 'And it wouldn't surprise me if it's going to be targeted at the first and deputy first ministers.'

'We should go to Stormont tonight and find out what's going down tomorrow. Because clearly it's something big!'

'I want to know what's happening on the republican side,' Lorna dropped herself back down on the rug, crossed her legs and continued to stare into the fire. 'They're too quiet for my liking. And if they're receiving support from anyone, then this can turn into a bloody disaster.'

'I don't want to see a bloodbath. It can't be remembered as "Bloody Thursday".' Brendan sank down beside Lorna. 'But if the British want to make this depressing hole unstable to give it back to Ireland, they'll do so! If they're going to waste innocent lives as if everyone else is expendable, then I won't lose a wink of sleep over taking out whoever's behind it.'

Lorna looked at him, then back at the fire. She took in a deep breath then slowly exhaled. 'We'll go down tonight and have a good look around. See if there's anyone who shouldn't be there. Let's set our alarms for three a.m. We can get up, have breakfast then go.'

'I'm going for a swim before I go to bed,' Brendan said. 'I'll sleep better if I tire myself out first. Besides, my mind's racing and there's no chance I'll be able to sleep right now.'

Lorna liked the sound of a dip in the pool. Tomorrow, they could be dead - or in prison, which would be worse. 'I'll join you.'

# Chapter Fourteen

AT THREE IN THE MORNING, Brendan's alarm went off. His eyes shot open. His mind was already awake as if he'd never been asleep. He rolled over and found Lorna beside him. She was already awake, sitting up with her back resting against the headboard, staring at her phone, a distant expression on her face.

'Did you not sleep?'

'Woke about ten minutes ago,' she said, still focussed on her phone. 'Why would Irish Prime Minister Seamus Toner be arranging a visit to Downing Street next week.'

'That's weird. He never goes there.'

'Unless, he's going to discuss a proposition with the British.'

Brendan rolled off the bed and casually strolled across the room towards the ensuite, wearing nothing but his boxer shorts. 'You joining me?' He looked back at Lorna who was acting a little more shy than earlier when they'd kissed by the fire.

'I'll wait until you're finished.' She pulled the blanket back over herself, lying back down on the bed.

'Today's going to be a day to remember,' Brendan shouted, as he pulled the shower door open and switched it on. He stepped in, standing under the shower head, relaxing in the hot water until he began to feel drowsy, then he cooled the water down until the shock woke him up again.

Stepping out of the shower and into the room, he looked for the expensive navy suit he'd bought from the Moss store in Belfast. His father had always taught him a man in a good suit and who carried himself well, was a man to be respected.

Lorna rolled out of the bed and went for a shower. Brendan was surprised to find she'd had her pistol under her pillow. He looked at her. She looked back at him. 'When you've worked for British Intelligence for so long, and travelled the world to some of the most hostile places, having a weapon close at hand becomes as normal as having your phone.' She passed him on her way to the bathroom, stroking his arm. 'You'll look nice in a suit,' she smiled. 'Agent Cleary.'

'I'll go make us some breakfast.'

Brendan had prepared an Ulster fry. While sat at the table, they didn't know what to say to each other. They were still strangers in a sense; strangers that had been dropped into a political mess, perhaps set up to take the fall.

Hilton's phone beeped. Lorna snatched it up from the table as if it were a priceless document, ready to blow away in the wind. She checked the message: from Director General of British Intelligence. She looked at Brendan, shifted in her seat and grinned as she read it out to him. 'The Director General is leading a meeting with the Irish and British Prime Ministers tomorrow in London. He's told Hilton, or *us* that today must not fail. Everything's in place to make sure today is a day that will go down in Irish history.'

'This place has had enough bad history to last a lifetime. It doesn't need any more.' Brendan looked across the kitchen at a sticky note on the fridge. It grabbed his attention. He stared at it quizzically for a few seconds, then got up to take a closer look. 'Looks like my father was aware this was going to happen.' He ripped the note from the fridge and returned to the table. The note read:

*Brendan, don't let them break you. Go to our place. There, you'll find all the help you'll need. I'm sorry, son. I got you involved in this. If you're reading this, I'm already dead. I will have been murdered - at the hands of the very people you're now on the run from.*

As he read the last sentence out loud, Brendan's eyes filled up like glasses of water. 'I love you and I've always been proud of you.' He looked at Lorna, his face flushed, his breathing heavier. He handed her the note and she re-read it, shaking her head as she did.

'I don't know what to say, Brendan.' She handed the note back. 'I'm sorry.'

'It's not your fault, you didn't do anything.' He folded the note and slipped it into his phone case, behind Bobby's bank card.

'I know this changes everything, Brendan,' Lorna said, sounding like a councillor. 'But, we need to keep our heads cool. Doing something reckless isn't going to help us.'

'I'm not stupid. I know how to keep my head. Even more so now.' His glazed eyes looked deeply into Lorna's. 'And we've got all the help we need. If he knew this would happen, I'm sure whatever it is he's left us will help us get the job done.'

'Where is this place?'

'It's where all my training took place. Where I spent all those summers, sweating, crying, screaming for it to stop.'

Brendan paused, looking as if he was reliving his adolescent nightmare.

'Your father wouldn't have wanted you to give in to any torture you may receive; we both may receive if we're caught. What he put you through those summer months, is exactly what he and I have gone through in our training.'

'Let's get to Stormont and see what's going on down there. Today will just be the beginning of this, so we can get down to my old training ground after we find out what's about to go down!'

# Chapter Fifteen

THE DARK COUNTRY ROADS had an eerie stillness to them. Almost as if the ghosts of those who'd perished to Ireland's civil unrest were coming to watch, fallen spectators, waiting to see if they had more joining them. The sound of the car's air conditioning pumping hot air was a constant reminder of the silence in the car. Brendan was behind the wheel, tapping it with his fingertip while humming, perhaps in a bid to appear confident. Lorna sat to his left, repeatedly checking her phone as if Hughes were going to message her from beyond the grave.

'So,' Brendan finally broke the silence as he guided the car through the quiet streets of outskirts Belfast. 'What are you going to do when this is all over?'

'No idea,' Lorna said. 'I guess it all depends on what the ending looks like. Perhaps run for prime minister. Couldn't be much worse than the one we have now.'

'Rather you than me,' Brendan said, as his phone's sat nav alerted them Stormont was approaching. 'You fancy using some of those tranquillisers to get in?'

'Of course,' Lorna said, checking her pistol was loaded. She then fitted a silencer. 'I wouldn't have a problem using real bullets.'

'And you said I'm meant to be the wild one. All we need to do today is gather as much info as we can, then find someone we can trust. We need some serious evidence to make them take notice. We've got statements from Hilton. We've got photos of the drop. Some politicians close to guns and paramilitaries would be great.'

'If the police service is involved, there may well be undercover army involved. Other agents. This whole thing stinks right through government and we can't trust anyone, Brendan. It is us against the world, until we get enough dirt to clear our names.'

THEY CRUISED ALONG the Upper Newtownards Road towards Stormont Estate, quickly becoming aware of the heightened police presence around the grounds. Years ago, perhaps that level of security was expected, but not when Northern Ireland had long since seen peace. Both leading political parties were working in relative harmony. The guns and bombs, had on the most part, been taken out of Irish politics.

'It's like a flashback to *better* times,' Brendan said sarcastically. 'Let's see what happens here, then.'

They approached the security gate.

'They'll recognise the car as MI5 property. Hopefully!' Lorna gripped her pistol.

Brendan pulled up to the security barrier. The guard craned his head out of the hut. Looking at the registration plate of Hilton's vehicle, he waved them through. The barrier lifted. Brendan looked at Lorna. 'This is too easy, I don't like it when it's too easy.'

'Don't be so negative, Brendan.' Lorna was quick to correct him. 'We need all the luck we can get.'

He led the car up to the main car park. Both wondered what to expect. Bombs. Bullets. They'd intercepted one van, but another five were out there still, filled with some very nasty stuff that had the ability to bring Northern Ireland back in time a few decades.

'We'll go for a nice walk around the grounds before the rain comes on. It's sure to arrive at some point,' Lorna half joked. 'This is the Emerald Isle, after all.'

Stepping out of the car, feet crunching on the gravel beneath, Brendan whispered. 'These stones will give us away.'

'If there's going to be an attack on the politicians today, where would they attack from?'

'Well, if the police are helping them. If the British government is in on it, then they can pretty much do it wherever they want. Why not just do it discreetly, like poison them. It would be cleaner, and more sophisticated.'

'Yes, but it has to look like the work of one of the paramilitary groups if it's to bring back the mistrust between the two communities. We have catholic churches being attacked around the province. That's the beginning of it.'

They took a walk around the main building. It was five-thirty in the morning and the chirping of the birds was the only thing that gave away the arrival of another day. And if Brendan and Lorna were to be unsuccessful, it would undoubtedly go down in history as another day in the violent, somewhat unstable history of Ireland.

As they approached the endless flight of steps that led up into the building's entrance, they heard the distant hum of a petrol engine in the distance.

'He's up early,' Brendan said, as they both looked around to find a flashing amber beacon moving towards them. A Belfast City Council ride-on lawnmower was drawing a neat line along the sloping grass to the entrance. 'I've got an idea about how we can get into the building without looking out of place.'

'You're joining the maintenance team?'

'There's a maintenance block around the back of the building,' Brendan said. 'If they're all out working in the grounds, we can get into the office and wait for them to come back.'

'Security must be watching the estate, Brendan. Especially if they've been told to be vigilant today.'

'Okay, we'll go back to the security hut, act stupid, say we're lost, then put them to sleep with one of those darts you love so much.' Brendan gestured at Lorna's bag. 'You can become estate security and I'll prepare to trim some hedges.'

'Let's go.'

Upping their pace back towards the car, Lorna's bag sounded. It was Hilton's phone. She pulled it out. A message read:

*Where are you? We have everything set for today. Don't mess up. If you do, it'll be disastrous for all of us.*

'Sounds like Hilton's got quite a bit on today,' Lorna joked, as she dropped the phone back in her pocket.

Brendan opened the car door and jumped in behind the wheel.

Lorna was warming to him. She placed her soft hand on top his as it rested on top of the gearstick. The two of them hadn't had time to bond, but it was apparent one was forming all the same.

Pulling up to the side of the security hut, Lorna got out just as the hut's door opened. The security guard stepped out, a cigarette sitting between his lips. He was short and over-weight. He moved at a painfully slow pace, scratching the side of his head that looked as if it were without a neck, just placed on top of his shoulders.

'Those things are bad for you,' Lorna said. He grunted, then sniggered. Before he could strike a light, she shot him dropping him instantly. 'Right, grab him.' She gestured for Brendan to make himself useful. Brendan grabbed him by the scruff, pulling the dead weight up from the ground, ripping the top three shirt buttons of the guard's shirt.

Stepping into the hut, Brendan dropped him down onto the floor beside a messy office desk. On the desk lay a copy of the Belfast Telegraph. Open on page five was an image of the very security gate they now had access to. Upon closer inspection, the story described a need for heightened security at Stormont Estate for the arrival of British Prime Minister Nigel Thorn which was due to take place in the coming weeks.

'Think you should have heightened security now, not tomorrow or next week.' Brendan spoke to the newspaper as if advising the journalist. 'This is a very well thought out plan.'

'Crafty bastard.' Lorna spoke in disgust, as she checked the live feed on a screen displaying twelve security cameras. She now had eyes on the estate. 'Right, Brendan. We haven't got time to mess about. I'll stay here and control the gate. You go and help cut the grass or something.' She looked around in her bag. 'Put this in your ear so we can communicate whenever we need to.' She handed him a tiny round object.

'Cool. Think of everything, don't you.' He inserted the device and nodded.

# Chapter Sixteen

TIME: SIX FIFTY-FIVE. Brendan got to the maintenance hut with some assistance from Lorna being the eyes of the estate, steering him away from the maintenance crew. Approaching the steel container, fit to go on the back of a lorry, he almost expected to walk in and find a handful of smuggled immigrants. Instead, an empty office. A fusty smell lingered, coming from the faded burgundy sofa that occupied the corner below a poster of glamour model Grace J Teal in all her glory. 'She's nice,' Brendan said. 'Wouldn't mind an evening with her.'

'Pervert.' Lorna's voice came through his earpiece. 'All men are perverts.'

Brendan ignored the remark as he approached the desk. An A4 sized diary lay open. Written in blue pen were the daily jobs of litter picking, brushing, hedge trimming and lawn mowing. Written in red ink was a list of priorities that needed to be completed before the end of the day, with a note of extra support brought in if needed. It was as if they wanted the estate to look it's best, like the eyes of the world would be on it and standards might be scrutinised.

Brendan checked the rota to see who was working. To his surprise there had recently been a lot of recruitment. 'Lorna, we have a brand-new maintenance team, according to the last few weeks of the staff rota. Everyone – including the supervisor –

has gone through a speedy training programme to bring them up to speed with the dos and don'ts of the job.'

'That's interesting,' Lorna said sarcastically, 'perhaps they were useless. Or else, the new recruitment team are here temporarily to create something quite spectacular – or even explosive.'

Brendan grabbed the staff training file from the top of a dusty filing cabinet. The new starters had names he'd never heard of before. Of course, if this was a scam to get them into the grounds, real names wouldn't be used. 'None of these guys are members of any...' he trailed off.

'What was that?' Lorna said. 'Didn't catch the end.'

'None of these guys have used their own names. Obviously, it would be stupid to do so. But, one of them is named "Alex Higgins" and I know a guy who was a die-hard snooker fan. He always called himself Alex Higgins in the club he ran. If it's him, he's Jonty's right hand and will have taken Jonty's place since I forced the teeth down his throat.'

'What's his real name?'

'Graeme Whiteside. He struts around Belfast like he's Al Capone,' Brendan said. 'If he's here on the payroll, then the entire maintenance team will likely be a new wing of the Belfast UDA.'

'I still don't think this will be a sniper job. I'm hoping at least they plan something less dramatic than a bombing. Something more sophisticated, and clean. They might have grown in class with some financial backing from the British government.' Lorna paused, then cleared her throat. 'Hilton's phone has received a message. It says *Bloody Thursday is upon us!* This is coming from the Director General.'

Brendan checked his gun was still in his pocket. 'Right, I'm going to throw on a pair of overalls and get out into the grounds.'

'Be careful,' Lorna said.

Brendan lifted a pair of oily overalls off a hook behind the door and stepped into them. He grabbed a high-vis jacket and a sweaty old baseball cap, then stepped out of the office. According to the rota, there were six men on shift, with another two starting at nine. By nine, the MPs and MLAs would be in their offices setting up for the day.

Making his way around the grounds of the estate, Brendan captured the scent of freshly cut grass, a smell that took him back to his childhood years in his capacity as the trainee super-agent that his father was shaping him into. Or as Brendan thought: a load of nonsense; at least until he'd met Lorna. He looked across the staff car park and spotted a car he'd recognise anywhere. A blue Subaru Impreza with a white stripe through the middle of it, sitting on a set of gold alloys. 'Well, Mr Higgins. Glad you're actually working for a living now.' He took a photo of the car.

Following the directions of Lorna as she scanned the grounds, Brendan made sure to avoid the other members of the team. He was guided on a long route through the garden's trees, towards the back of the building. Unsure where to go or what to do, he stopped at the recycling area about fifty yards from the main building.

'Lorna, any chance of some...'

Before Brendan could say another word, Lorna interrupted him. 'Brendan, we have a well-built member of the maintenance team going in the front door. They're letting the cleaners in. Go in with them. Don't talk to anyone, in case someone recognises you, but go in and see if there's anything dodgy going on in there, and...' Lorna trailed off. 'I see a van that looks awfully like one of those from the port. It's just pulled up to the gate.'

Brendan's heart began to race. 'Let them in. Don't speak to them. Just raise the barrier and let them through. I'm on my way up the main steps now. Going to go in and look around. Keep your eyes on them. Let me know where they go.' Brendan flicked the collar of his overalls up and pulled down the peak of his cap.

Progressing up the steps that became famous for the many occasions both the DUP and Sinn Fein leaders stood – apparently – shoulder to shoulder, Brendan thought about what a spectacular spot it would be to assassinate the leaders of Northern Ireland – for the world to see. Brendan thought about how it was more like something from a Godfather movie. Only this wasn't a movie, or entertainment. It was real life, and if an assassination on the DUP and or Sinn Fein leaders were to take place, the people of this part of Ireland would undoubtedly be plunged into another storm of sectarian bloodshed.

He got to the top of the steps and looked at the six pillars of the front of the building: each representing one of the six counties of Northern Ireland. Entering the building, he almost felt like he was entering Belfast Crown Court with the shiny floor tiles and magnificent Greek classical architecture. Right down to the squeaking of his shoes as he walked, he was almost ready to step in front of a judge. It wouldn't have been the first time. But if they were caught, being in front of a judge would be the best-case scenario.

'Brendan, that van is now pulling up to the steps you just climbed. Someone's jumped out of the back and is headed your way. They've even waved over to one of the maintenance crew who wanted their attention.'

'Okay, I'm going to say hello to him,' Brendan said, as he went to the vending machine beside the lift.

'Be careful, Brendan. Don't start something with this guy that you can't finish. We'll be in a mess if you cause a scene now.'

'I can be tactful, don't worry.' Brendan pulled a bottle of water out of the vendor.

# Chapter Seventeen

BRENDAN OPENED THE bottle of water and poured half of the contents into his mouth just as a dark-haired well-built man wearing a black polar neck, cream jeans and black boots came through the front door. He looked around the area, his twitchy movements revealing his current state of mind. Why was he nervous? He spotted Brendan and ran over to him, looking relieved. But before he could speak, Brendan spat the mouthful of water into his eyes. His natural reaction was to put his hands up to wipe the water away. Brendan took the opportunity and swung his right boot straight between his legs, connecting with his groin area. The guy crouched over, then dropped.

'Very sophisticated.' Lorna's voice came through Brendan's earpiece.

'Got the job done, didn't it?' Brendan responded, as he punched the guy on the jaw, knocking him unconscious. The guy's head hit the tiled floor, two of his teeth scattering across the polished floor. Instinct kicked in and Brendan removed the man's belongings: an iPhone, a wallet and handgun. Looking in the man's wallet, Brendan discovered he was Andrew Davidson from Ballymena. He had an Apprentice Boys badge tattooed on his right hand, and UDA tattooed across the knuckles of his left.

Brendan dragged the unconscious Davidson across the squeaking floor towards the vacant disabled toilet next to the vending machine.

Lorna came back in his ear. 'Brendan, we've got a British army helicopter just landed in the grounds of the estate.' She sounded as if she was watching an action movie unfold while eating popcorn.

'Who arrives in a chopper at this time of the morning?'

Lorna replied, this time slowly emphasising every word. 'I know one of the men who just got out. His name's Jack Smith, and he's one fucking hard ass. He leads the training in the SAS.'

'What does the SAS have to do with loyalist paramilitaries attacking politicians at Stormont?' Brendan remembered back to his childhood, when his father spoke about how the SAS were responsible for the Bloody Sunday and Ballymurphy massacres when innocent – mainly Catholic – civilians were gunned down on the streets. 'They're here to create more mayhem? I'll give him mayhem.' Brendan scanned the area, wondering where this Smith was going to appear. He knew he'd have his hands full. He didn't know exactly what he was capable of, but it appeared he possessed some very useful skills that his father had kindly battered into him.

'He's just given something to one of the maintenance men: a bag. He's getting back into the chopper. I've got photos of the exchange. I don't know what they've been given, but whatever it is, it's important enough for the highest skilled British forces to deliver it. It's something we should get our hands on.'

'Where are they headed with it?' Brendan locked the disabled toilet from the outside, leaving Davidson inside.

'Make your way back to the maintenance office. That's where they're headed. But be careful, Brendan. They're in numbers.'

Brendan shrugged off the warning. Making his way towards the maintenance office, he produced his pistol, checking the silencer.

As he got closer, he heard shouting. One of them was furious at another. Lorna came through.

'Brendan, don't go in there. Come back to me and we'll watch them from the security cameras.'

'I can handle myself, don't worry,' Brendan said, as he neared the office. The door was closed but an open window made it easy for him to figure out the conversation. 'Just you watch my back from the security cameras.'

'What are you doing?' Lorna asked, as Brendan crept up to the open window. Listening to the conversation, it was clear the gang was planning an assassination attempt on the leader of Sinn Fein and acting Deputy First Minister Sean McManus. But the reason for the attack was that MI5 had supplied a recording of a conversation. McManus was doing a secret deal with the British and Irish governments to move Northern Ireland away from the UK and unify the thirty-two counties of Ireland using a rigged referendum.

Upon hearing this, Brendan knew a lot of hard-line loyalists would take this as a breach of the peace between the two communities.

'Well, if MI5 wanted to wind the UDA up, it's gone about it the right way,' Brendan whispered. He continued listening. To his surprise, the group was talking about taking out the leader of the DUP and acting First Minister Andrew Coleman, too, for knowingly agreeing to the idea. Coleman had apparently sold out the loyalist community who had elected him into power. All for a nice sum of money. They would live the rest of their lives in the lap of luxury, whilst the loyalist community would have to get used to the idea of being governed from Dublin.

'I think we've underestimated the severity of all this,' Brendan said, as he walked away from the offices. 'I'm coming to you.'

Lorna grunted. 'When I watched my superior's brains splat all over the windscreen of my car, I knew it couldn't get any worse. You've got a clear walk to the hut, but don't hang around. It's eight twenty-five and the traffic is starting to flow.'

Brendan upped his pace to almost jogging speed, not wanting to attract too much attention. He looked around the well-maintained gardens of the estate. 'It looks like they've done a good job of the maintenance duties.'

'Let's save the jokes for later, Brendan. We've got a black Mercedes Benz, an S Class pulling up to the gate. McManus travels in that car, doesn't he?'

'Yes.'

Brendan walked along the path of the estate's main entrance, facing the Mercedes, trying not to look directly at the car. His face would be known to McManus and possibly the driver. Then he clocked the driver's face, recognising him in an instant.

'Marty Collins is driving that car,' Brendan hissed, putting his head down, forcing his hands into his pockets. He was fifty yards from the security hut. 'He's involved in the New IRA. They're the combined RIRA and the CIRA.'

'Brendan, if they shoot Marty Collins, along with the attacks on all the Catholic churches, this will act as a catalyst to New IRA recruitment.'

'Like the Bloody Sunday and Ballymurphy massacres.'

'This place is going to be a warzone.'

Brendan stepped into the security hut. 'Right, what the hell are we supposed to do?'

# Chapter Eighteen

IT SEEMED AS IF A DARK cloud of violence was about to descend over the already grey sky of Northern Ireland. Upon checking the local news, the UTV Live news reporter said the graves of the ten IRA hunger strikers had been destroyed. Twenty Gaelic sports clubs were no more. Thirteen Catholic churches had been burned to the ground. Six Catholic men and a couple had been shot dead while walking the streets. No information was given in about who'd carried out the attacks. No organisation had claimed responsibility. But two dead bodies found tied up at Saint Colm's Catholic church close to Ballycastle were said to be members of the UDA.

An uneasy stillness filled the air in the office. Brendan watched video footage of the carnage. Lorna gasped, shaking her head. It was easy to block out what was happening to their lives. They could run away and hide forever. They had the funding to do it. But neither of them looked like they were willing to.

'I'm going to wipe every one of these bastards out!'

Lorna gripped his hand. 'We'll do it together. Being smart and not getting caught. But first, we need to stop whatever's happening here today. Christ, all we need is one of the leaders being shot.'

They continued to watch the morning updates. Every channel was the same and would be the same for the rest of the day. Undoubtedly there would be a public condemnation from both the First and Deputy First Ministers.

'I can see it now: a shoulder-to-shoulder outcry from both Sinn Fein and DUP leaders. Probably at the steps to...' Brendan trailed off, stumbling across the most likely answer that was to go down at Stormont.

'What?'

'A public assassination of the two leaders, that's what the loyalists are planning!'

'It would make sense. The loyalists always wanted to make a bigger name for themselves, always living in the shadows of the IRA. Now's their chance. And with the backing from the British government, who's going to stop them?'

'We are,' Brendan said.

Just as he said this, an entourage of black Range Rovers with blacked out windows pulled up to the entrance. Lorna lifted the barrier. The six SUVs stormed in, making their way towards the front steps.

'Even if we stop whatever happens here today, enough damage is done to rattle both communities. We might already be too late,' Brendan said.

'We can still save two lives and prevent it from getting worse.' Lorna checked her phone. 'We might not have enough evidence to bring the British government into question for it though.'

'We'll get that from London,' Brendan said. 'If we stop these attacks today and get to the house in Donegal, hopefully we can find out what my father left. Then we can go to London and find Smith. I don't care if I have to storm parliament to get what we need. I'll create the most dramatic public show the world has seen if I have to.'

'We may have to,' Lorna mumbled, her gaze fixed on the CCTV monitors. The second from front Range Rover presenting the First Minister with the Northern Ireland Secretary of State Joanne Whitehall.

Hilton's phone went off on the desk. Lorna picked it up and read the text. She laughed without humour. 'Well, we can confirm what they're planning.' She glanced at Brendan then back at the phone. 'An assassination of both leaders during a televised speech this morning.'

'We need to know where from. And we need to get our hands on that package the helicopter dropped off earlier. Whatever it is, it's important.'

Adrenaline was kicking in. The next few hours, would be the most explosive they'd seen in their lives. Their lives, and those of many others would be impacted. The end would depend on how the two of them acted. Both with different drivers. Brendan – motivated by the murder of his father. Lorna – still trying to get her mentor's burning corpse out of her head. But both were running to save their lives.

'I'll get back to the maintenance office. You stay here,' Brendan said.

'According to this rota...' Lorna ripped a document from the notice board, 'my shift ends in half an hour and the next guard comes to relieve me.'

'Okay, even better. Let's dump our friend...' he gestured towards the unconscious security guard, 'in the boot of the car. Leave a note for the next person to arrive.' Brendan stopped himself. 'No...'

'I'll just stay here and put the next one to sleep when they come in. It's better if I wait here. I can be your eyes around the grounds.' She turned and looked at the monitors again. 'And my eyes are telling me you should make a break for it now. They're all leaving the maintenance hut. Hopping back onto their mowers. 'Go now, Brendan. Stay connected.'

Brendan made his way out of the hut, feeling as if the eyes of the world were on him already. He made his way along the tree-lined road, weaving in and out of the natural cover, staying out of everyone's sight.

With Lorna's all-seeing eyes watching over him, he had to stop and hide as one of the mowers zipped past. After a stealthy progression, he finally reached the maintenance hut. Only it wasn't vacant. He could hear a voice coming from inside.

He stood behind the door, and after a minute of listening, he realised the conversation was one way. Only one voice was contributing to the discussion, meaning the silent contributor to the conversation was likely on the other end of a phone, and not physically in the room.

Brendan checked his pistol was ready to fire. But just as he was about to barge in, Lorna hissed in his ear for him to stop. 'Brendan, *don't* go in there without knowing what's behind that door.'

'They're on the phone,' Brendan whispered. 'I'm pretty sure there's only one person in there.'

'Well then, if they're on the phone, that makes it even worse.' Lorna laughed sarcastically. 'Come on, Brendan, you're smarter than that.'

'What?' Brendan had no idea what she was getting at until it clicked. 'Whoever's on the other end of the phone will hear it and give us away!' He slapped his palm into his forehead as if to call himself a dumbass.

'Bravo!' Lorna said.

He crept back away from the door. As he did, the talking finished, and footsteps could be heard getting closer to the door. 'Fuck, they're coming out.' Brendan raised his hand, pointing the pistol straight at the door. The door opened.

'What the...' Brendan froze.

'Brendan?'

'Bobby?' Brendan stared at his uncle, Bobby looking back at him like a rabbit caught in the headlights. Brendan found himself in a moral dilemma. His aunt's husband and chief ass-kisser to the late Damien Cleary Sr was at his mercy. Brendan felt reluctant to pull the trigger.

'Brendan, put the gun down, son.' Bobby slowly raised his hands. He stood around five feet nine inches and was so thin that if he stood behind a lamppost, he'd disappear. 'Don't shoot, Brendan. Let me explain.' Still with his hands in the air, his phone rang in his left hand. 'I need to answer that.'

'Brendan, what's happening?' Lorna's voice came through Brendan's ear, bringing him back into the present. Brendan lowered his pistol. Then, just as Bobby went to answer, he raised his aim again and put a bullet in his uncle's head. Bobby's lifeless body dropped to the ground.

Brendan stepped closer to Bobby, his pistol dropped to his side. 'You shouldn't have got involved.' He stood over Bobby's body as dark red blood pooled. The phone continued to ring. Brendan picked it up. The name "Boss" flashed on the screen. He ignored it and dropped it in his pocket.

After dragging Bobby's body into the office, Brendan found a sniper rifle on the desk - and, to his delight, the bag that had been dropped off by the chopper. About to grab the bag, he hesitated and pulled his hand back. Growing up in Belfast taught people one golden rule to a longer life: stay clear of unknown packages.

'Brendan, the next security guard has arrived. He's very kindly logged into his email account for me. He's the supervising security guard and was responsible for employing all the current staff.'

'What a nice guy,' Brendan said sarcastically, eyes fixed on the bag. Tilting his head as if it would somehow figure out what was inside. It didn't. 'I've found the bag. But I don't know what's in it, and with my experience growing up in Belfast...'

Lorna interrupted. 'I know, don't just jump on it if you want to keep your limbs.' She paused. 'Hold on a second,' she whispered. 'I've got an email saying the package is being delivered. It has everything signed and agreed between the Irish prime minister, the minister of defence, Northern Irish first and deputy first ministers, and finally by the British prime minister.'

Brendan grabbed the bag and opened it. He pulled out a brown envelope with "CLASSIFIED" in bold red across the flip. Inside there was a two-inch-thick stack of word-processed documents. He quickly flipped through, seeing references to his father, granddad, Bobby, Lorna and himself. *It was all a set up*

'Lorna, these documents involve us!' Brendan's heart began to race. She didn't respond. 'Lorn..'

She stopped him there. 'Brendan, we've got BBC crews here. There's a lot of activity up here. I think it's about to get a lot busier.'

'No shit.' He threw the documents back into the bag and took it with him. 'I'm on my way back to you now. In Bobby's car.'

# Chapter Nineteen

JUMPING INTO BOBBY'S car, Brendan felt a pinch of nerves, sending butterflies fluttering around his stomach. The deeper into this they got, the more trouble they were getting in. There was *no* turning back now. He'd now killed. His hands were soaked in blood. But preventing innocent lives being lost, was his justification. But when you're fighting against the government you have nobody to turn to. The only thing that would keep them alive was staying out of the government's grasp. Being caught, they'd surely both be six feet under like Brendan's late grandfather.

Making his way towards the front entrance, he passed BBC, UTV, RTE and Sky News reporters, crews from all the big broadcasters, making for the steps to Stormont. He pulled up to the security hut. As he stepped out of the vehicle, the sound of a chopper circling around the estate cast his mind back in time, a depressing memory of the past when British army helicopters plagued the Irish sky.

'Hurry up and get in,' Lorna hissed, from behind the door. 'I don't know how much time we have but it'll not be long. And if that chopper's in the air on the orders of British Intelligence then it'll be more interested in spotting us than the would-be assassins.'

'What do you suggest?' Brendan asked, checking the CCTV. 'We've got some MLAs already giving their usual speech of condemnation.' On the screen, members of Sinn Fein, the DUP, SDLP and UUP all spoke in front of different cameras, being showcased on various channels. When asked the question about what happens now to the current talks taking place, the member of the DUP said that will be disclosed when Coleman and McManus address the public. When asked when they'd be addressed, the MLA responded saying that the two leaders were in a brief meeting before taking any questions. In fifteen minutes to half an hour the First and Deputy First Ministers would be out to talk to the press.

'Good, at least we know when it's due to happen.' Lorna set three black Glock 17 pistols down on the desk. She looked at Brendan. 'This may turn into a warzone very soon. We're going to need all the help we can get. Have a scan through those documents, see if there's any mention of an attack point. And be aware that if it's a long-distance sniper job, it'll be harder to identify.'

Brendan dropped himself into the office chair, scanning through the documents. He paused when he saw his father's profile: a summarised version of Damien Cleary's adult life. Brendan slowed down and read the first page of the classified data. According to what was written, the deceased was in possession of information that could bring into disrepute not only the British government, but also it's allies.

'What have you found?' Lorna asked, realising Brendan was totally engrossed in whatever he was reading. She stepped around from the side of the desk. Looking over his shoulder she put her hand on his arm. 'Come on, let's go.'

Brendan dropped the stack of paperwork on the desk, stood up, turned and pulled Lorna in for a kiss. She hesitated for a second, then yielded. After a moment of serenity, they parted. She looked down at the stack of paper to find plans of the building. Stormont's parliament building was on an exploded map with indications of roof access.

'A bit of Irish luck,' Brendan laughed, as he clutched Lorna again. Looking at her, he smiled. 'Let's go hunting for some gunmen.'

'It's going to happen any minute.' She grabbed the pistols. Handing Brendan an over-sized pair of sunglasses and the security guard's jacket, she grabbed another. 'Well done, you're now a member of the Stormont security team.' She pushed him out the door, pulling on another jacket and hat. She pulled the door closed and locked it, putting a sign on the door saying *Checking the estate, back in ten minutes.*

They walked along the narrow path that lined the right side of the estate's access road – a mile long straight line, heading in only one direction: the main building. The crowd of reporters and politicians was growing. Security could be seen floating around in the grounds. All looking like they could be the would-be killers.

'Why do I get the feeling this is going to be a greater massacre than we expect?' Lorna said. She was looking at one of the security guards standing at the entrance steps.

'Nothing would surprise me,' Brendan said, scanning the area, paranoia kicking in.

They made their way towards the crowd, mingling with camera crews. Momentarily, an atmospheric silence was cast over the estate. A spooky feeling, as if at a funeral. Nothing but the distant hum of the chopper's propellers. Then it was real. First Minister Coleman and Deputy First Minister Mc-

Manus appeared from the front doors of Stormont. Making their way down the steps, they provided each other with the usual small talk in a bid to look like buddies. Brendan and Lorna continued to watch, scanning the grounds. Police crews were now mingling amongst the crowd. Security guards were keeping their distance.

A noise came from the entrance to the grounds. A deep thud. Then the ground shook. They both spun around. The security hut was on fire. The police and most camera crews ran in the direction of the carnage.

Lorna's head shot from left to right. towards the hut and back to the ministers. She gripped Brendan's forearm, her nails digging into his skin. 'It's a diversion,' she shouted. 'We need to keep our eyes...' she was cut off by two guns shots. The cracks sent echoes through the air. A second later, screams came from the dispersing crowd around the ministers. Speechless, Brendan and Lorna both looked at two suits lying across each other, their dignity stripped from them.

'Christ!' Brendan shouted. He and Lorna both sprinted towards the scene, being stopped by a group of security guards who'd formed a protective circle around the bodies. The chopper that had been circling the grounds landed on the grass. Six British soldiers jumped out, spreading out and canvassing the gardens.

Still staring at the corpses, Brendan tugged Lorna's sleeve. 'Let's go, we gotta get outta here. We can't be seen.'

Lorna turned and led the way towards the maintenance hut for their car. But it wasn't long before a PSNI officer shouted for them to stop. They both broke into a sprint. The officer ran after them. Calling for support, the officer was now one of three chasing them down. There was no escape for them.

'The chopper, quick,' Lorna shouted. 'I'll fly.'

'Can you fly that thing?' Brendan shouted.

'Just get in the chopper, Brendan,' Lorna shouted with less than fifty yards from them and three PSNI officers. A gun was fired, Brendan felt fiery pain in his shoulder. He jumped into the back of the chopper, clutching his wound. Lorna jumped into the pilot's seat as another three shots struck the pilot's door window. She wasn't hit but didn't like the idea of the shooter having a couple more attempts. She started the engine and within ten seconds the aircraft was making it's ascent into the air, everything below them getting smaller.

The chopper took off, leaving Belfast in the distance.

'Fly us over the Cave Hill mountain, towards Antrim. We'll grab a car. We need to get to Donegal.'

# Chapter Twenty

DITCHING THE CHOPPER on a derelict patch of land, behind an old abandoned shed constructed from corrugated iron, they ran towards a house they'd seen just a half mile back. Brendan hot-wired the white Land Rover parked in the driveway and they made their way towards Donegal.

Neither of them spoke during the two hour journey. Lorna drove. Brendan checked his wound. Just a scratch.

Seeing the sign for Donegal brought a mixture of emotions for Brendan. He'd not been at the house since those teen years. Certainly not since his father had disappeared and his unease was evident.

As they pulled up to the pebble-dashed white walls that surrounded the coastal estate, Brendan felt as if he were travelling back in time. The creak of the black gate as it opened, the feel of the bricks as the car made it's way up the driveway and even the sound of birds chirping as if singing a welcoming melody all added to the vivid memory of where Brendan was moulded into the man that was somehow destined to impact the future of Northern Ireland.

He entered the digits to the pass code protected lock on the front door. The door opened. Brendan went in first. Lorna produced her pistol as if danger was around the corner.

'Are you sure nobody knows about this place, Brendan?' Lorna looked as if she were ready to start shooting the shadows on the hallway's magnolia walls.

'I'm sure. He wouldn't have left a message for us to come here if he had any concerns.'

Lorna lowered her weapon. 'Perhaps you're right. He wasn't just any operative. But before we do anything, let's have something to eat, I'm starving.'

'I'll rustle us up something,' Brendan said, making his way through the five-star hotel style living room – high ceilings, three bow windows draped with cream curtains and marble floor which squeaked with every step he took. 'Go and check out the rooms upstairs. See what he's left for us.'

He walked into the kitchen, feeling like he was stepping back in time. The stainless-steel fridge-freezer still held a painting Brendan had drawn for his homework in primary five. It was a picture of himself and his father outside a house with a red car. He remembered drawing it. He also remembered why he drew it. It was his dream at that time that his father would stop disappearing for months on end. The car was the Ford Sierra Cosworth, always roaring up the driveway of the family home to signal the return of the mysterious Damien Cleary.

Feeling slightly conflicted by the memory, Brendan stood, puzzled, tilting his head as if looking at it from another angle would somehow give him a different answer, perhaps a different reality than the reality he was living. But of course, it didn't. It did however present him with a new-found appreciation for the message behind the drawing: a wish that his father would come home and stay home. Now, Brendan would use this drawing as a reminder of what the intelligence service had done to him. That young boy whose only wish was for his father to come home. Now he'd never be home again. And Brendan was ready to die in his attempt to stop the same people from creating any more broken families. The world didn't need another drawing like the one he'd just ripped off the fridge door. He folded it and tucked it neatly inside his wallet.

Pulling the fridge door open, he found nothing but bottles of water and cans of Pepsi. That wasn't enough. 'Come on, dad,' he mumbled to himself, as he pulled a can out and cracked it open. He reached down into a cupboard directly to the right of the fridge. 'Better.' He pulled an unopened packet of pasta and two in-date tins of salmon.

After putting the pot of water on to boil, he sat at the breakfast bar in the centre of the room. Checking the BBC news on his phone, he noted the entire website was awash with stories of the carnage that took place in the Stormont estate. Northern Ireland's two political leaders gunned down in front of the world's media.

'We've failed,' he mumbled to himself. Continuing to watch video feeds of global condemnation from the world's leaders, Brendan could not take a word any of them said seriously. After the cold-blooded murders of the past few days at the hands of British government, confidence in the influential people of the world was non-existent.

Lorna walked in with a laptop bag. 'This is all I could find.' She sat down beside Brendan. Setting the bag down on the desk, she smirked at him. 'Have a look.'

Brendan took the bag and pulled the laptop out. He looked at the boiling pot. 'We've got pasta and salmon.'

'I'll sort the pasta out,' Lorna said, as she approached the cooker.

Brendan opened the laptop. The screensaver was a photo of Brendan performing the centre splits all the way to the ground with his arms folded and his eyes closed, looking at peace.

'That looks painful – the splits,' Lorna laughed. 'But you looked like you were enjoying it.'

Brendan laughed. 'After a while it became easy. The first time was deadly. I couldn't walk properly for days.'

He guided the mouse over a folder named "Brendan" and left clicked. It opened a list of documents set in date order. Dates started from the 1980s right up to the current year. Spotting a video recording he clicked on it. It was his father, speaking to him from the grave.

'I'll give you a moment to listen to this, call me in when it's over.'

'We're in this mess together, Lorna. You don't have to leave. Whatever he has to say, is as much for you as it is for me.'

She approached him, sitting down on the stool next to him. Brendan pressed play. They listened to the recording. It lasted three minutes and eighteen seconds. The video explained how the accompanying documents would be enough to incriminate the prime minister, the Secretary of State for Northern Ireland, the head of British intelligence and would filter down through the government. But what took both Brendan and Lorna by surprise was the involvement of the Irish government. It appeared all three governments were willing to sacrifice the lives of many, to line their own pockets. At the end of the video, the late Damien Cleary gave the two enemies of the state a set of resources that would equip them with what would be a battle with the world's superpowers to not only clear their names, but to save countless lives in Ireland. They were astounded at the amount of information Damien Cleary had in his possession.

Brendan opened a documented list of everything they'd need, and a plan B.

The list consisted of: Five bank accounts – each with a balance of five million, fake passports for both Brendan and Lorna. A suitcase full of weapons, communication equipment, mobile phones, and suits. A contact list and schedule of the personal secretaries to the British prime minister, Secretary of State for Northern Ireland and the head of British intelligence. Recordings of conversations held between the Irish prime minister, the first and deputy first ministers of Northern Ireland and the British prime minister. What was most surprising, was the conversation between the British and Irish prime ministers. The conversation advertised the willingness of both heads of state to set up the conversations with Northern Ireland's two leaders and feed these to the paramilitary groups. This was to label the leaders of the DUP and Sinn Fein as sell-outs. Piss off both sides of the community and offer up a fabricated chance for the IRA and UDA to unknowingly take out the Stormont leaders and re-ignite their war for independence from the other's rule.

'They'll hang for this,' Lorna said. 'They've played everyone for their own gain. And I'm guessing your grandfather was murdered because they knew he had information that would tell the truth about what's just happened. I think he knew a lot of what your dad knew, and the British government wanted to start getting rid of people who it seen as a threat.'

'We'll finish it for him.' He looked at Lorna.

'You know they'll be hunting us,' she said. 'We'll need to disappear until we can get this information into the hands of the right people. I hope you're ready for an international game of manhunt with the targets on our backs.'

'Fuck it. We're dead either way! Let's go down with a fight.'

# Chapter Twenty-One

AT FIVE FORTY-FIVE Brendan's alarm sounded. He sat up and grabbed his Samsung, wanting to launch it at the wall. Their cabin on the P&O Dublin to Liverpool ferry was barely big enough for two kids never mind two adults. It was the early hours of Friday morning, less than twenty-four hours after Bloody Thursday earned itself an entry into the archives of Irish history. Another dark day that was about to lead to a rise in sectarian violence in Northern Ireland, after so much work had been done to restore peace. Twenty-four hours was all it would take to wipe out a couple of decades of peace work and building bridges. The 1998 Good Friday Agreement was a day the people of Northern Ireland, Republic of Ireland and Britain had hoped would put an end to it all.

Brendan sat up, placing his bare feet on the worn carpet. The boat rocked. He placed his head between his legs, wishing he was on solid ground. He looked up at Lorna who was in the opposite bed, still asleep. Her Glock slipped out from under the pillow as she rolled over to face the wall her bed lay against. That pistol was a glimpse into the life they'd both been forced into. They had all the resources to run and hide for the rest of their lives. Why didn't they?

He was about to get up and wake her until she began to mumble something. He couldn't make out what it was. Her breathing became shorter, more rapid. She made a noise that could only be described as a squeal kept behind her lips, then she started to cry. Still feeling wobbly on his feet, he stumbled towards her bed and sat beside her. Her cheeks were moist. He put his hand on her shoulder. She flinched and turned to face him, her eyes suddenly wide open.

'Are you okay?'

She sighed. 'I'm fine.' She wiped sweat from her forehead and rubbed her eyes with her knuckles. She propped herself up on her elbows. 'What time is it?'

'Nearly ten to six.' He examined the cut on his shoulder.

'You'll live,' she groaned.

'Wish I could say the same about Smith,' Brendan said. 'He'll not be breathing much longer.'

'We need to be very careful. Smith is one crafty son of a bitch. He...' she trailed off, her eyes looking at the wall as if willing it to come alive.

'What?'

'He uses the underground tube. Hughes always took the piss out of him, calling him a coward. He didn't trust anyone, and believed he'd be safer in public than in a car.'

'Trust issues?' Brendan joked.

'Because he's an untrustworthy bastard. But that'll be a good place for us to look for him.'

Brendan lay down beside her, looking at his phone. BBC news was consumed with what had happened in Northern Ireland.

*Stunned Is The Feeling In Northern Ireland* was the title of the story.

'It's pretty much the feeling everywhere.' He frowned, handing the phone to Lorna. He jumped up off the bed again.

'I'm grabbing a shower.' He paused at the bathroom door and looked back. 'We need to fix this mess.'

After his shower, Brendan tidied the room while Lorna went to freshen up. She took a little longer, so he made himself useful by putting the room in order. He checked the bag of guns, each fitted with a silencer. His training in Donegal all those summers, during his teenage years, was finally making sense. He always thought it was punishment. He hated it at the time and hated his father for it. Now he was slowly coming to appreciate it all. He grabbed the Glock G43 slimline pistol, taking it apart in seconds then re-assembling it. He cast his mind back to how Damien Cleary Jr would time him, recording his times and noting how much he'd improved between the start of the twelve-week Irish summer holiday and the return to school in September.

Lorna stepped out of the bathroom, a cream towel covering her torso, and another wrapped around her head. 'You're like a little boy playing with his new toys.'

'Happy birthday to me, then,' Brendan said, pulling the slide back and dropping the bullet into his hand.

Lorna shook her head. 'Are you ready for some breakfast? The food on these things is like shit, but I'm starving.'

'Get dressed and we'll get out of this cramped space, then. I'm feeling claustrophobic.' He threw the Glock back into the bag and zipped it closed.

Lorna took the towel off her head, revealing chin-length black hair in complete contrast to the straight blond hair that had previously reached halfway down her back. Brendan sat on the bed, waiting for her to put on her jeans and hoodie. She dressed her face in the usual makeup, but with more gothic colours. She then blew him a kiss.

'You look nice with your hair short,' he said.

She grinned at him. 'You should to do the same. I like your beard and those long curly locks, but you need to change your appearance, too.'

'You want to take it off for me?'

'Take your tops off, then. Unless you want an itchy back all day.'

'I guess breakfast can wait,' Brendan said, as he pulled his black hoodie and t-shirt off.

# Chapter Twenty-Two

AFTER CHANGING THEIR appearance, they cleared the cabin, never to return. On the deck below, they joined the queue of half-asleep passengers lining up with their trays in hand.

'Reminds me of being at school in the canteen, waiting to fill my stomach with a greasy Ulster fry – my morning pleasure.'

'Easily pleased, then,' Lorna said, not really paying attention to him, *or* the words that came out of her mouth. 'I see our mug shots are all over the news. Not surprising.' She stopped and shook her head. 'Listen to this: these terrorists are wanted on suspicion of orchestrating the attacks and assassinations of the first and deputy first ministers of Northern Ireland. They are considered armed and extremely dangerous. If you have any information on the whereabouts of either of them, contact the PSNI.'

'Let me see.' Brendan snatched her phone. 'That's not even a good picture of me.' His voice dripped with sarcasm. 'Well, at least it's not all bull-shit. We are armed and dangerous.'

'But directed at the people who're really responsible for this.'

Brendan approached the hot plates. Even with the mayhem that was now their lives, he managed to smile at the sight of proper breakfast. Both he and Lorna filled their plates with as much food as possible.

Taking a window seat in the corner of the dining lounge, they watched the boat cut through the freezing cold Irish Sea leaving a white trail of bubbles behind.

A thirty-inch plasma mounted on the wall facing them displayed the news. Stormont was now a crime scene. Blood stains on the steps and chalk outlines where the bodies had dropped was an image that the people of Northern Ireland would remember for a long time. Brendan stared at the screen as the camera zoomed closer. He didn't blink until Lorna placed her hand on his.

'You okay?' she asked.

He nodded and hummed. 'You?'

She looked down at her plate, nodding.

'What about your family? Have you had any contact with them?'

She shook her head, cutting through a bacon rasher. Dipping it into the ketchup, she placed it in her mouth. 'Nope.'

'Do you have anyone that may be able to help us?'

'I've a sister who lives in Chelmsford, east of London. I'm pretty sure she's worried sick. But...'

'You don't want to get her involved?'

She shook her head, piercing the egg yolk with a fork full of soda bread. 'This bread isn't bad.' She looked at him, forcing a smile.

'Isn't bad? That's an understatement.' Brendan did the same with his soda bread and egg yolk, smiling at her as he put the food in his mouth.

They both listened to a couple at the next table talking about what had happened at Stormont. The man had an English accent, from the Liverpool area. The lady's accent was similar to Brendan's. They were debating the likelihood of British soldiers going back onto the streets of Belfast. They both believed there would be a need for it, if there was another night of violence that had dominated the local news. The guy mentioned how he didn't trust the news and his faith in UK politics was pretty much non-existent. The lady was less interested and declared that people needed to "wind their necks in" and just get on with their lives.

Brendan and Lorna exchanged glances, both seemed to find some humour in the fact that the two alleged culprits were sitting at the next table.

'If I didn't know better, I'd say there was government involvement,' the guy said. 'I mean why the hell would the two people responsible for it all be right there at the time of the incident? It doesn't make sense.'

'What are we going to do today when we get home? Fancy giving the grass a cut?' The lady responded.

Lorna laughed. 'Looks like not everyone gives a shit about it.'

Brendan looked out the window as the floodlights of Liverpool's port reflected off the water. He released his tightly fisted hands and watched the blood turn his white knuckles red again. 'Coffee?'

Lorna just nodded as she checked her phone.

Standing at the coffee machine, Brendan noticed a homeless man in the reflection of the machine's brass housing. His beard hid his entire face, wrapped in a torn and faded brown blanket from the waist to the neck. He shivered as if he were sitting on a block of ice. Brendan caught a whiff of him as he passed, before returning to Lorna. He concluded that he'd rather be dead than like that guy. Some animals had better living conditions. For a moment he found some appreciation for his own, far from perfect existence.

'What are you grinning for?' Lorna said, as he set the two cups down and slid back into his chair.

'I'm just glad I'm not like that homeless guy sitting over there.'

'It's one of the more depressing things about life in a developed country. It shouldn't be accepted.' She lowered her head, hovering her nose over the steam as it rose up from the cup. 'Coffee – one of the most satisfying aromas I've ever experienced.'

'We'll have to make a trip to Italy when we're done in London. Try out some proper coffee.' Brendan followed in Lorna's example in taking in the sweet aroma. 'If this mess has ruined our lives, then the least we can do is make the most out of the money we've been left.'

'You know whatever happens, Brendan, our lives will never be the same. Even if we clear our names it'll...'

'*When* we clear our names.'

'... never be the same.'

Brendan blew in his cup and took a sip. 'Let's just catch this bastard Smith and we'll figure out what to do after that.'

IN THE QUEUE OF IDLING vehicles waiting to disembark the ferry, Lorna drove and Brendan rode shotgun. Their BMW X6, one of a few vehicles left at the house in Donegal, was a comfortable drive from the west coast of Ireland to Dublin port on the east coast.

It was seven forty and the sun was just beginning to rise. The sky was a light pink shade merging into a light blue. The car followed an Alpha Romero right up until the junction for the M6 Birmingham. It was a four and half hour journey from Liverpool's Royal Albert Doc to London, so they'd agreed to drive half way each.

While Lorna was focussing on guiding the car through the early morning rush hour, Brendan revised the emails that they'd sent to their private accounts. In the next twenty-four hours, there would be an invaluable compilation of evidence to incriminate the people who set them up.

The morning news in Northern Ireland was awash with discussions about the terror attacks across the province.

'I think most people are shell-shocked about what's happened. They're struggling to believe it,' Lorna said, as they listened to the Radio One host take calls from people in Belfast.

'Probably because it's a load of bollocks,' Brendan said. 'I wonder was it really a paramilitary who shot the leaders, or a British hit man.'

'It could very well have been a British assassin. We'll soon find out.'

After driving under a red x in the lane she was in, Lorna slowed down as the next lane was closed, followed by the third. Just one lane was left open due to an accident, almost bringing the morning traffic to a standstill.

'I'm going to sleep,' Brendan said. 'Wake me up when it's my turn to drive.

# Chapter Twenty-Three

BRENDAN WOKE TO THE sound of the car door slamming shut. Lorna had stopped at a motorway service station. Pump six was filling the BMW with a full tank of unleaded. He looked around, feeling groggy. He went to scratch his head, then remembered there was little hair left after Lorna had her fun with the scissors.

He flipped the sun visor down and slid the mirror cover across. 'Shit. My head will be freezing.'

'We'll get you a hat,' Lorna shouted in the window. 'You want a coffee?'

He nodded his head while rotating it to get a look at himself from different angles. 'Throw in an extra shot.'

'You'll need it, you're driving the rest of the way.'

He got out to stretch his legs. The cool air was refreshing. His heart began to race as a marked police car drove into the station, stopping at pump seven, directly behind the BMW. He inhaled, causally spun around on his heel to face the petrol station just as Lorna came out with the coffees.

'You ready to go?' She was good at acting casual. Brendan nodded his head and walked around to the driver's side of the car. He didn't speak. His accent was too distinguishable. All eyes were not only on Belfast right now, but those same eyes were on the lookout for a couple. A couple which consisted of an Irish man with a Belfast accent and an English lady with a London accent.

Getting into the driver's seat, Brendan adjusted his position, then the steering wheel. Before he started the engine, he blew on the coffee and took a sip. He swallowed, then grimaced. 'How many extra shots did you put in that?'

'Two.' Lorna smiled. 'I thought you could do with a kick to wake you up.'

He laughed. 'This'll do it, I'm sure.' He started the engine. 'Okay, where are we going? We can't just drive to the London headquarters of British Intelligence and expect to just stroll in with a big bag of guns and bad intentions.'

'We'll ditch this car in a housing estate in Chelmsford. We can get the bus from there into London.' Lorna blew on her coffee and took a swig. She gazed at her new appearance in the sun visor's mirror. 'I've bought us day tickets to use the tube.' She laughed as she brought the cup back to her lips. 'It'd be lovely if we could bump into Smith on...'

'What?'

'If we can back-trace his steps from the stop closest to the headquarters, we...' she trailed off again as she pulled her phone out again. 'You know what, Brendan. With any luck we might not need to go directly to the headquarters.'

'Don't place your hope on any *Irish* luck,' Brendan joked as the car merged onto the M40 London bound. 'I'm pretty sure that's just a myth.'

The car picked up speed, doing seventy-five mph before they even left the slip road.

'Don't be revving the shit out of this thing. We should have enough fuel to get us to Chelmsford, but not if you drive it like a rally driver.'

'You're the boss,' Brendan joked as he brought the speed back down to seventy.

'Okay, if we can find him getting on the tube after work, we may be able to follow him home. I want to see how this bastard lives with all his dirty money.'

'Are you sure we can just follow him home? I'm sure a guy like him would have measures in place to make sure things like this don't happen.'

'The good thing we have on our side is that I know all the protocols to keep our agents safe.'

'You're quite useful then.' Brendan teased.

'I can hold my own,' Lorna replied, not giving Brendan the pleasure of reacting to his remarks.

The journey to Chelmsford was a quiet one. The sunlight was blinding. Brendan needed shades to protect his sleep deprived eyes.

An hour before reaching the destination, Lorna fell asleep with her head against the passenger door's tinted window, her head rattling in unison with the vibrations coming up through the car. Brendan focussed on the road ahead, the physical road, and the psychological road. Perhaps the road trip would prove an easier journey than the road his mind was facing.

Reading a sign that said "Welcome to Chelmsford" he reached over and gently shook Lorna awake.

'What?' she groaned.

'We've arrived. Where will we leave this thing?' He pulled in to the bustling carpark of a fast food restaurant and convenience stores, giving Lorna a moment to regain her senses.

She sat up in the seat and yawned. 'We can walk from here. We need to take the Greater Anglia platform one at Chelmsford station. That'll take us to London's Liverpool Street. From there, we'll have our day tickets to get us around on the underground.'

She checked her bag then looked in the back. Gesturing to the bag of guns on the seat she said, 'perhaps keep them out of the way. We'll be better carrying less.' She craned her head over to Brendan's side, looking at the petrol gauge. 'Better fill the tank again before we leave. When we come back here, if we do, we may need to get as far away as possible.'

'Okay.' Brendan started the engine again. 'There's a petrol station just around the corner.'

After filling the car with another fifty pounds worth of unleaded, they took off on foot towards Chelmsford's Abellio Greater Anglia. The wind constantly reminded Brendan of the fact that his shoulder length curly hair was a thing of the past.

'It is still bothering you?' Lorna asked, seeing him rub his hand across his head to generate some heat.

'What, the head?' Brendan laughed. 'I'll survive. You should have seen some of the extreme things I had to do in Donegal all those years back.' Brendan threw the gym bag over his shoulder as it continued to slide down his arm.

'Give me an example? Entertain me.'

'Okay.' Brendan dropped his head and watched his feet as he walked. Deep in focus trying to think of something. 'The first year of my training was when I was ten. I always had a fear of snakes and spiders. There was a giant, room sized tank... shit it was horrible. It was swamped with those slimy little bastards, slithering all over the place.' He paused for a second. 'He said if I wanted to survive, I'd have to get the container full of food that was lying in amongst them.'

'And you were only ten?'

'He spoke so casually at the time, saying he had to rush back to Belfast and would be back within the week.' He laughed, shaking his head. 'It's amazing the things you can do when you set your mind to it.'

Lorna agreed. 'I know exactly what that training does to you. They want to bring you to breaking point. Then go a little further.'

'He always told me I'd be grateful for this training one day. I remember after that first summer, crying myself to sleep every night. When I went back to school after that summer, everyone in my class knew something had happened to me. And every summer it just got harder. But even though it got harder, it's strange because I found it easier to cope with the thought of it. By my fifth year of going down there, it was just a formality. I didn't care. I was more like: "wonder what he's got up his sleeve this year" and he would always surprise me. It was the psychological training that was the hardest. But the other training: the martial arts, the weapons, the shooting, even the study – it was all good.' He looked at Lorna. 'Maybe that's why he made me go through the tougher training first, get it out of the way.'

She nodded. 'I can't believe you were put through all that when you were so young. That's designed to break grown adults, not ten-year olds.' She held his hand. 'One thing I don't get is how someone like that ended up in such a mess in the cell after a drunken brawl outside a Kebab shop.'

'I stopped giving a shit. The great Damien Cleary Jr disappeared almost seven years ago, just before my twenty-first birthday and I had no guidance other than that of my grandad. And there was only one-person people feared more than my dad, that was the one person he feared...'

'*His* dad,' Loran finished.

They approached the artistically built Abellio station. The time was twelve thirty and the next transit was due to arrive in thirty minutes.

Entering the café, they were both overwhelmed by the aroma of ground coffee and the sweet smell of strawberry jam. After going to the toilet while letting Lorna join the queue, Brendan took a window seat facing the room and the door. Another thing drilled into his sub-conscious by his father – always keep your back to the wall and face the room. You want to know the minds of every person in the room.

He watched Lorna order them both an English tea and a cherry scone. The music in the café was faded, barely noticeable in the background from the noise of clattering crockery, joking kids, and exasperated parents trying to get their children to settle down; perhaps excited to spend the day in London.

Lorna approached the table and set the tray down. She took the seat beside Brendan, not wanting to have her back facing the room either.

'Ever been to London?' She handed Brendan a cup and a scone.

He shook his head. 'First time.' He gestured over to a group of excited teenagers. A mixture of boys and girls, black and white. 'Why am I not as excited as them?'

'I doubt they're going to London as fugitives, going straight to the government that's after them.'

He laughed. 'What I would give to be a normal teenager agai...' he paused. 'Actually, I never was a normal teenager.' He pierced the roof of the scone, watching the steam rise from it.

'Okay, we'll get to Liverpool Street around one thirty.' Lorna did the same with her scone. 'Smith usually works until six. So, he'll be in the tube around six thirty. We've got a few hours to kill.'

'Fancy a day at the Ritz?' Brendan joked.

'You've never been to London, but you know the Ritz?' She laughed, putting a fork full of scone in her mouth. She hummed while nodding her head.

'Afternoon tea at the Ritz might be a nice first experience.'

'Okay, once we get to Liverpool Street, we'll kill a few hours at the Ritz.' She laughed. 'You don't seem the type.'

# Chapter Twenty-Four

AT ONE THIRTY-FIVE, they arrived at London's Liverpool Street Station. Stepping off the bus, Brendan had never seen such a sea of people. It was literally a fight to get through. Angry commuters were pushing people to get out of the way. And what was more surprising was people didn't react to it. Clearly it was an acceptable way of behaving in London.

'Right, the way to the Ritz?' Brendan shouted in Lorna's ear. 'Lead the way, because this is like a maze to me.'

Lorna laughed. 'First of all, we should go get some nicer clothes, my handsome Irishman.' She linked her fingers between his and led the way. After thirty seconds of pushing and shoulder barging through the crowds, they arrived at the concrete steps that led them down into the underground. She pointed at a map sign on the wall - *West Ruislip Ten Stops To Oxford Street.*

After waiting ten minutes on platform three, the train rattled into the station, squealing to a halt. The automatic doors flung open and commuters spilled out. Once on the train, they sat on the hard plastic seat that were as blue as the morning sky. Lorna played on her phone, while Brendan watched the screen as it displayed each stop: Bank Station, St Paul's, Chancery Lane, Holborn Underground Station, Tottenham Court Road and finally their stop – Oxford Circus Underground Station.

Getting up, they joined the stampede out the door. Seeing the rush of commuters disembarking from the London transport facilities would lead one to believe that there was a fire on board.

They climbed the twenty something steps to ground level, fed their cards through the barrier and were soon on their way out to the main street.

After a five-minute walk, they arrived at number four hundred Oxford Street. Reiss Selfridges stood, with elegantly dressed dummies modelling in the windows.

'You know, a cheap suit would be good enough, I don't really give a shit about fancy clothing,' Brendan said, hands in his pockets.

'If we're going to eat at the Ritz, if we're going to be framed by a corrupt government, if we've got millions to spend in the name of bringing down that government,' Lorna looked at Brendan, 'we're sure as shit going to do it in style.' She took him by the hand. 'Come on, let's at least have a little fun with this money.'

Entering the shop, they were hit in the face with hot air being pumped out of the heating vents. Lorna led the way. Brendan was more interested in getting his hands around the throat of Smith and listening to him beg for mercy while giving up the rest of the people involved.

Lorna went straight for the men's section. Brendan trailed behind her. His body was there, but his mind was somewhere else. He looked at the clothes. Suits priced at six hundred pounds and climbing. He spotted one of the dummies wearing a hat and scarf. Then he woke up.

'You can make us look good all you want,' Brendan said as Lorna lifted a slim-fit suit and held it up in front of him. 'But we should also get some accessories to hide us in public view.' He gestured at the hat.

'Good idea.' She handed him the suit. 'Go and try this on. Think it might fit you.'

'Serbelloni?' Brendan read the tag. 'Anything Italian must be good.' He took the hanger and strode off to the cubicles.

Half an hour and over twelve hundred pounds later, Brendan walked out of the shop dressed in a grey three-piece suit linking arms with Lorna wearing a low-cut black V-neck dress. With a pair of heels on she stood level to Brendan's six-foot frame.

They made their way back towards Oxford Circus and saw their faces plastered all over the papers on a nearby newspaper stall. Brendan reached up and checked his hat, making sure his sunglasses were still firmly in place. Paranoia was kicking in. Every step they took in London was a step closer to getting their hands on Smith.

'You're quiet,' Lorna said. 'Feeling like a small fish in a big pond? Used to being a big fish in a smaller pond?' She poked him playfully.

'I don't give a shit where I am. Belfast, London, Milan, New York – I can feel at home anywhere. Whenever you can get that kind of mindset, you can face anything.'

'Guess you can thank your terrifying snake experience for that.'

Entering the underground again, they took the train for Brixton and after one stop and one minute they were at Green Park. A one-minute stroll got them to number one hundred and fifty, Piccadilly, St James. There it was: The Ritz, London. It wasn't like Brendan hadn't travelled the world and seen some of the most beautiful places known to man, but he *was* impressed with this.

Taking their seats in the dining room, they both laughed.

'This will be quite a story to tell one day,' Lorna said.

'To who? Our kids?' Brendan grinned.

She smirked at him. She showed him the screen of her phone. An image of them both. Wanted by the authorities. 'We're the most wanted people in this part of the world right now. And we're sitting here, pampering ourselves in the finest of outfits, about to be waited on, hand and foot.'

'It's an insane story,' Brendan agreed.

A tall thin waiter came over to inform them that they could help themselves to the buffet or order and have whatever they like brought over to them. He spoke as if he was addressing the royal family. No slang, or accent.

Brendan gestured towards Lorna. She wanted the full table service.

After they'd pretended they weren't wanted fugitives and spent the last hour and thirty minutes rubbing shoulders and sipping tea with some of London's wealthiest, they left to do the job they'd really come to do. Arriving back in the underground, the human traffic was heavier than earlier, if that was even possible.

'We'll get off at London Bridge Station, it'll be around six fifteen by the time we get there.' Lorna said as their lift arrived.

'Are you sure he'll be there?'

'As sure as I can be.' She stepped into the packed carriage, followed by Brendan. A well-dressed man who looked like he'd spent the day on the London Stock Exchange or in the director's chair in one of London's biggest banks sat reading the paper. He had it up in the air, directly in front of his face. His face couldn't be seen behind the paper, but Brendan and Lorna's mugs were in plain view for everyone to see. Perhaps it was a good thing none of the other commuters bothered looking.

'Where'd you like to disappear to?' Brendan whispered in Lorna's ear.

'I don't care.' She stared at the front cover of the Telegraph. 'Once we get our names cleared and everyone who's played a role in this is brought to justice, we can go anywhere.'

'Early retirement sounds good to me,' Brendan said.

The sign came for Jubilee London Bridge. They got off. It was six fourteen. An accurate approximation by Lorna. Now all they had to do was wait.

The next forty minutes were the longest of the day. The endless rattles of trains rolling into the station; people jumping on and off. Brendan sat on one of the grey plastic chairs, his backside growing more uncomfortable by the second. His hands joined, resting on his legs, wondering if the next person would be the one who chose to ruin his life for some cash.

Lorna sat with her legs crossed, her suspended foot bouncing up and down. Together they looked like a couple who'd missed their lift to a prestigious ball.

'Where does he live?' Brendan broke the silence.

'I'm not sure where, but it's not far from here.' She laughed. 'Hughes always called him a lazy bastard because he used the tube when he could easily cycle or even walk. He's...' She trailed off. Her eyes fixed on a tall, thin male in a navy pinstripe suit walking with an extra spring in his step - unusual for the time of the day when most people were tired. He looked excited about something. Perhaps even proud. 'That's him,' Lorna hissed, as she looked down at the ground. 'We're in business.'

Brendan glanced at the man. He stood at the edge of the platform as if he had to be the first one on the train. Brendan had other ideas. 'How about we just go up and throw the bastard onto the tracks when the train pulls in?'

'That'd be too easy,' Lorna said. 'I want him to pay. If nothing else, I want to find out the name of the bastard who pulled the trigger and killed Hughes.'

'I hear the train coming.'

They both slowly stood up, completely ignoring their target. As the train squealed to a halt, they stepped in. Brendan stood, holding onto the hand rail; Lorna sat down. Smith was in the next cabin. Brendan had his back to Smith's cabin but could see him in the window's reflection. The train left the station. It went past Southwark Station, Waterloo Underground and Westminster Station.

'He'll change trains at the next stop. Get ready,' Lorna said.

Smith got off at the Greenline Richmond Station. It was clear whoever he was on the phone to was taking his full attention, making it easier for Brendan and Lorna to tail him. He was completely oblivious.

They jumped on the Richmond after him. Five stops and eight minutes later he got off at Gloucester Road.

He walked north on Gloucester towards Cromwell Road then turned left onto Victoria Grove. Finally reaching Victoria Road, they watched as he stopped in front of shiny black railings. He opened the gate and went in.

'You know, this was called the UK's most expensive street three years ago,' Lorna said.

'I'm sure he can afford it, the little deal he's done with a select few would pay for this house nicely.'

'We can't just go knocking on his...'

'Would he have all the evidence we need to finger everyone involved and clear our names? Prime minister including?'

'That's a good question,' Lorna said as she grabbed Brendan and pulled him in close. She planted her lips on him just as a black Ferrari 458 roared out of Smith's driveway. She glued her face to Brendan's as the sound of the 4.5 litre engine roared passed them. 'Bastard or not, he's got good taste in cars.'

They both watched the rear end of the Italian supercar turn out of the street, the red lights getting smaller with distance.

Lorna let go of Brendan. Both froze for a second. Looking into each other's eyes. The emotion in the air was tangible.

'Let's take a stroll past his house, see what's in there,' Brendan said. He took Lorna by the hand and led the way. The orange street lights pierced the darkness along the footpath. As they passed the railings of Smith's property, they could see all the lights in the imposing property were still on - lit up as if Smith wanted to use up all the electricity in the city.

'Nice car collection,' Lorna said, as she admired the grey Aston Martin and White Range Rover Sport in the driveway.

'I'd bet my life that he's not going too far,' Brendan said, crossing the road to get a closer look at the property. 'We should wait here until he comes back and get him as he opens the front door. He won't see us now it's dark.'

Lorna shrugged. 'We've nothing better to do than to wait.'

'Great, he's even left us a nice little bench to sit on.' Brendan spoke mockingly. He gently opened the gate, leading the way along the grey bricked driveway, around to the front of the Range Rover. The bench was surrounded by flowers. Brendan gestured towards them, 'maybe use them for his final resting place

# Chapter Twenty-Five

SEVEN THIRTY-TWO, THE rumble of the Ferrari could be heard three streets away, the engine getting louder as it pulled into the street and finally, the driveway. Brendan pulled his pistol out and checked that the silencer was secured. He looked at Lorna. 'You want to record this?'

She shook her head. 'And let you have all the fun?'

The thud of the car door slamming shut was followed by Smith's whispers. From the darkness of where they sat, they watched as his shadow grew longer on approach.

Brendan raised his pistol, ready and willing to put a bullet in Smith's head, but not until they got what they came for.

'What the fuck do you mean you still can't find them?' Smith fought to keep his voice at a whisper. 'You better find them, we need to find out what they know. Or it'll be all of our heads.'

Brendan looked at Lorna. 'Sounds like we're making people nervous.' He looked back in Smith's direction.

Smith was forcing his hand into his inner jacket pocket, almost as if he was trying to push the contents out through the bottom. 'Just find...' he said, finally pulling a key out. The call ended. He inserted the key into the lock. Brendan and Lorna jumped up from the bench and approached him silently just as he turned the lock of the door. He lowered the handle and took one step in. Before he brought the second foot in, Brendan had him by the back of the neck, dragging him into the hallway. Lorna followed and shut the door.

'Good evening, Agent Smith,' Lorna said, as he frantically tried to wrestle with Brendan. Brendan threw him face first into the wall. While still holding him by the back of his shirt collar, he dragged him into the living area, bowling him down onto the leather sofa.

With his nose bleeding, Smith turned, pushing back into the sofa as if trying to get away from the pair. Like a cornered rat. 'What the fuck is this?'

'Aw, come on, don't act stupid. The size of this house, and the cars you have parked outside prove you're not.'

'You're...'

'Brendan fucking Cleary, or thanks to you, the most wanted person in the UK right now.'

Smith didn't respond. He just kept his hands in the air, blood running freely down his face onto his lips.

'At least now you can tell whoever you were on the phone to, that you've found us.' Lorna sat down beside him, still pointing the camera.

'What do you want?'

'What do you think?' she said, tapping on the phone. 'We want a full confession that you set up Hughes to be murdered and you framed us for the murders of Northern Ireland's First and Deputy First Ministers. You've brokered a deal that will make you all very rich. You, Prime Minister Thorn and Irish Prime Minister Toner.'

'What? This is preposterous. You two are insane. Put that bloody gun down and I'll let you both walk out of here without any...'

Brendan shot a hole into the sofa, just a few inches away from Smith's head.

'Your dad really did teach you how to shoot,' Lorna grinned at Brendan.

He smiled at her.

'We want names... of everybody involved in this whole thing. We want to know everything, from the prime minister's involvement, right down to the scumbags who attacked all the Catholic churches and GA centres,' Brendan said. 'Once we have that, we'll leave. I don't give a shit what you do after that. You can run and hide like the worm you are, or you can stay and face the music.'

'He's going to run,' Lorna confirmed.

'As long as we have evidence to clear our names, I don't give a shit.'

'Okay, okay.' Smith sat up straight on the sofa. 'I'll tell you what you want to know, but on one condition...'

Brendan shot another hole in the sofa, this time on the other side of Smith's head.

'Okay, okay. It was all Hughes' fault...'

'What do you mean, Hughes' fault?' Lorna punched him on the mouth. 'You have the cheek to talk about a man who's head you had blown off?'

'Hughes brought to my attention the possibility of a scandal that dated back to when the troubles began. He found evidence of secret talks between the Irish and British heads of state. At the time, they were going to create mayhem on the streets of Belfast and Derry. The Irish government was meant to step in at the time of the Bloody Sunday Massacre. The British Prime Minister knew his time in power was coming to an end and he wanted a nice retirement fund. The Irish Prime Minister was going to buy the six counties back...'

'How?' Brendan sat down on the recliner facing Smith.

'With a rigged election. We were going to agree on an all-Ireland referendum which would have been a majority catholic vote. The British prime minister retires with a healthy bank account and his Irish counterpart would go down in history as the man who unified Ireland.'

'Why didn't it go ahead?' Lorna said.

'According to the documents that Hughes discovered, someone on the Irish side foiled the plot and the Irish prime minister dropped out. But of course, by this time, the people of Northern Ireland were already emotionally involved. We couldn't just close the case. Catholics were joining the IRA and Protestants were being sworn into the UDA, UVF and whatever other group was forming.'

'And what, so the current British and Irish prime ministers thought they'd have a go?' Lorna asked. She stopped the video and emailed it to herself and Brendan.

Smith started to cry. 'I'm sorry.'

'No, you're not!' Lorna said. 'You're sorry you got caught.'

'What are you going to do with me?'

'That depends on how useful you are,' Brendan said. 'I can't promise I won't kill you. But if you do exactly as we say, and prove to be a useful resource, well, you'll have a much greater life expectancy.'

'Okay, I'll do whatever you want.'

Lorna strolled over to the fireplace. 'Where are your wife and kids?' She lifted a family photograph off the mantel.

'They're at the other house. They know nothing about this house yet.'

'So, they don't know where you'd get the money to buy something like this.' Lorna set the photo back down again. 'Well, at least you had the decency to keep them out of it.' She sat back down again beside him. 'Pity you lot didn't offer the same courtesy to Hughes' or Brendan's family - or mine.'

'Right,' Brendan said, growing agitated. 'Where are these documents that Hughes gave you? I want everything you have. And access to all the prime minister's intel, too. This is going to clear our names.'

Smith started sobbing again. He looked like a helpless, weak little man, not the man who was in charge of British intelligence.'

'It's back at my office. But of course, you two don't want to wait until tomorrow and go there when there are people everywhere.'

'Of course we don't,' Lorna agreed. 'That's why we're going there now. The three of us. We'll give Brendan a nice little tour of the headquarters.' She spoke sarcastically. 'It'll be even more special, being night time and nobody there but us.'

'Come on, Lorna. Don't be stupid, you know there's security there,' Smith said.

'Don't you worry your little head about the security, because you're going to get us in. If an incident were to occur and bullets started flying, we'd be using you as a shield.' Brendan stood up and buttoned his jacket. 'So, Mr Smith, it'll be in your best interest to get us in there without any problems.'

Lorna reached into her handbag. Pulling out a bunch of cable ties, she threw them at Smith. 'Tie one around each wrist. Then I'll tie them together.'

'And as much as I'd like to drive that Ferrari, it's probably better to use the Range Rover,' Brendan said. 'So where are the keys?'

Lorna pointed at the mantel. 'They're up there.'

Admiring the painting of Winston Churchill on the wall above the fireplace, Brendan snatched up the keys. He noticed Smith was looking past him in the direction of the wall. When Brendan caught his gaze, he blinked and snapped out of it. Brendan looked back at the painting again. 'You like it? Or do you like what's behind it?' Brendan walked back to the painting and lifted it up. A safe was fitted into the red brick wall. 'You sneaky little bastard.'

Lorna laughed. 'Well done, Holmes!'

'What's the combination.'

'1984'

Brendan punched the numbers in, lowered the handle and opened the door. He pulled out a diary and a plastic pocket. The pocket had files on Brendan, Lorna and Hughes. It included a twelve-page report with a signature at the bottom of each page.

'Who's signature is that?'

'I'd say it's that weasel Hilton's.' Lorna pressed her pistol into Smith's back.

He nodded his head.

'You want to drive? I'm looking forward to having a flick through this entertaining read to see what we've done,' Brendan said.

'Sure, I know these roads anyway.'

Lorna drove the car expertly through what seemed like a maze of roads, while Brendan kept Smith company in the back.

'It's amazing how creative this guy Hilton is.' Brendan quickly scanned the documents. 'He'd been spying on you and Hughes for months.' He looked at Hughes' file. 'Hughes was to be eliminated because he wanted to do something good.' Brendan turned and looked at Smith. 'Was the money really worth it?'

Smith sat with his head bowed, his chin in his chest looking at his bound hands. He didn't respond.

'You can pray all you want, it's not going to help you now,' Brendan said. 'If there is an afterlife, you're going straight to hell.'

'And the British and Irish prime ministers will be going with you!' Lorna shouted. She stopped at a set of traffic lights just before a turn onto Park Street, getting closer to the headquarters.

Brendan lowered the heavily tinted windows of the Range Rover, taking in the cool air of the night. They pulled up to the offices. Smith was still looking down at his hands as if he'd given up.

Lorna pulled into the car park and shut off the engine. She turned around and looked at Smith. Then she smiled at Brendan.

'What are you grinning at?'

'Well, did I mention before that me being an agent had some benefits?'

Brendan nodded his head. 'This is only the twelfth time, I think.'

Lorna grinned. 'The reason why that is relevant this very second is because: as an agent, we're all given access to the secret passageway. A way in and out of the building that nobody other than agents know about.' She looked at Smith. 'You should have grabbed your coat, Chief...' She opened the door and jumped out. Opening Smith's door, she grabbed him and dragged him out.

Lorna led the way. They walked along the front of the impressive grey building with windows scattered like dots across the front. It looked more like a medieval castle with its neoclassical structure, but it was only built in the 1930s.

Lorna turned and looked at Smith. 'Lead the way. It's your office.'

He looked at Brendan. 'Take the keys from this pocket,' he gestured towards the left side of his suit jacket. 'That shiny silver key that looks like a miniature saw, that's it.' He gestured towards a lock into the wall. 'It goes in there.'

'That's well hidden.' Brendan opened the door, barely visible in the wall. He wrinkled his nose at the fusty smell. The automatic lights came on within seconds of them stepping inside. It was like a normal fire escape but was unknown to the tax payer who funded it.

Smith led the way to the top floor of the eight-storey building.

Brendan checked his phone while climbing the stairs. A BBC news report displayed an update to the ever-unfolding story at Stormont. Two bodies had been found at Bobby's house. The blame was again aimed at Brendan and Lorna's apparent reign of terror in Belfast. Brendan snorted.

Lorna glanced at him. 'What's entertaining you?'

'We're now getting the blame for killing Hilton. His body was found at Bobby's.' Brendan looked at Smith. 'I'm guessing our friend here wanted to tie up some loose ends.'

Smith again kept quiet. He'd appeared to be someone who'd been caught and didn't feel the need to protest.

There were two doors at the entrance to the top floor. One was an emergency roof access to a helicopter pad. The second led into the offices.

Entering Smith's office, Lorna instructed him to go straight to his computer and fire it up. Once Smith had signed into his account, Lorna took over while Brendan kept an eye on Smith.

Lorna knew exactly where to look and pulled off details about past and future meetings. Who the meetings were with and the outcome of each. She looked at Brendan, a pearly white smile illuminating her face. 'Bingo. Come and look.'

Brendan joined her.

There was a detailed plan on who was doing what in Northern Ireland. Brendan opened a zip file sent from the prime minister. This file was a plan drawn up by the powers of state in 1970. It had been altered to be executed in today's political climate with a specified amount of money agreed on.

'Lorna, what we have here is something that's going to send the British and Irish prime ministers to prison for a long time.' He looked at Smith. 'Don't worry, we won't forget you, either.'

'What did you expect to do, just take your money and disappear?' Lorna said.

'Fake your death and run off into the...' Brendan paused as he scrolled down through the files. One of the files was titled "playing dead". He clicked on the file. A plan for First Minister

Andrew Coleman and Deputy First Minister Sean McManus to do exactly that was outlined. 'They're not dead, are they?'

'Who?' Lorna asked. She looked at the screen.

'Jesus fucking Christ, you're going to create a blood bath back home. People will be slaughtered, while you bastards jet off into the sun.' Brendan grabbed Smith by the throat, flipped his pistol around and sent five blows into his face. His lip and his nose bled, his right eye closed. 'Where the fuck are they?' He threw Smith down on the desk and put the gun to his forehead. 'You will die right here, right now, on your own desk if you don't tell me where they are.'

'Fuck you.' Smith spat his blood at Brendan.

'Check his diary, Brendan,' Lorna said. 'The diary we got from his safe. There's a reason why it was kept locked up.'

Grabbing the diary from the desk, Brendan flipped it open. Before he got a chance to flick through the upcoming dates, Smith spoke in a defeated tone. 'They're in a safe house in South London. They're staying there until their replacements have been appointed and then they're slipping into Europe.' Smith sighed. 'Well, that was the plan, anyway.'

'Who all knew about this?' Lorna asked, as if she was still struggling to believe any of it.

'Global politics is the biggest scam on the planet.' Smith laughed. 'We're all in it for money.' He laughed at the two facing him as if he was astounded at their naivety. 'You really believe politicians give a shit about saving the world? Look at the most powerful men in the world. They couldn't care less about the people.'

'Well it's time all you money-greedy bastards get what you deserved.'

Lorna laughed. 'The prime minister won't need to wait until the end of his term to stand down next year, then. He'll be doing life for murder.'

Brendan flipped through the diary. 'According to this, you're meeting with your boss and his Irish counterpart tomorrow.' Brendan looked at Lorna, then Smith. 'I think it's a good time for you to send your two accomplices frantic texts. Tell them you're all in deep shit. Say you've had to rush down to the safe house. Something has happened with the "ghosts". You tell them that they need to get down there. ASAP.'

'Brendan, we've probably got enough evidence here to clear our names.'

'No, I want to see them all in one room. Everyone who stood to benefit from this.'

Lorna looked at Smith then back at Brendan. 'Get this piece of shit back to his car. I'll scan this room for anything else.'

'I'll wait here and...'

'Brendan!' Lorna shouted. 'Do you trust me?'

Brendan wasn't used to letting someone stop him while he was talking, but Lorna was different. This was different. His whole life was different now. 'Of course, I trust you. We don't have anyone else, do we?'

'Then let me scan this room. I'll be faster by myself and without distractions.'

Brendan grabbed Smith. 'Let's go, we'll need to get you something for that nose bleed.'

They left the room while Lorna slid back into the desk chair and went back on the computer.

Ten minutes later, Lorna jumped back into the driver's seat of the Range Rover. The engine was idling, and the heating was pumping. The temperature was set at 21 and in view of the outside temperature of 8, she found herself glad of a pre-heated car.

'Okay, Smith.' She adjusted the rear-view mirror so she could look him in the eye as she spoke. 'Address?'

'Dean Street, East Farleigh, Maidstone, ME 15.' Smith sounded as if he'd almost had to drag the words out of his mouth.

Lorna typed the address into her sat nav. The estimated arrival time was one hour via the A2. They took off.

'How are we looking for petrol?' Brendan called from the back seat.

'There's enough,' Lorna said abruptly, sounding like it was all beginning to get to her.

'Are you okay?' Brendan asked.

'I'm just tired.' She fidgeted with the radio. Finding 97.9 – BBC Radio One, she turned the volume up to listen to the half-hour news broadcast.

'Okay, then. I'll drive. Pull over. You can sit in the back with Prince Charming here.'

Lorna pulled over and jumped out without even responding. Before Brendan knew it, she'd pulled open his door. She looked at him as if to say what are you waiting for.

'Are you sure you're okay?'

'I'm just starting to get a headache. I need to close my eyes.'

He didn't say anything, just got out.

Getting into the driver's seat, he guided the car back onto the road. Radio One was replaying interviews with people in Belfast and Derry. They all said there was a sense of uncertainty in the air. Stormont looked like a ghost town. And the media didn't help matters by calling yesterday "Bloody Thursday". Even though that's what it was, bringing back unsettling memories for the previous two generations. The new generation was fortunate enough to have grown up without the misery of the generations before. Now, everyone feared a return to the old days was just around the corner.

'How can you live with yourselves?' Brendan shouted. 'I swear to God, you'll all regret doing what you've done.'

Smith didn't respond.

Lorna didn't respond either.

Brendan focused on driving the car. Getting them to their destination.

# Chapter Twenty-Six

PULLING UP OUTSIDE the house on Dean Street, Maidstone, Brendan killed the lights, then the engine. The house looked like an oversized cottage. The long narrow front garden was lined with flowers. The lights were on. There was a black Toyota Landcruiser parked outside the front door. Not the type of vehicle you'd see two state officials travelling around in, but it would act as a good cover.

With the silence in the back, Brendan assumed both had fallen asleep. When he turned around, Smith was still staring at his joined hands, like a death row inmate trying to come to terms with his fate. But Lorna was looking straight ahead, her eyes wide and glazed. Brendan waved his hand across her face. She blinked and snapped out of it.

'Right, let's go,' she said, pointing her pistol at Smith. 'You try anything funny and I'll blow your head off. It's that simple. Do you understand?'

Brendan opened his door and stepped out. The air was noticeably colder than when he got in. He pulled Smith's door open. 'Let's go and say hello to your mates.' He pulled Smith out, giving him balance until he found his feet firmly on the ground. Lorna followed.

'Don't slam the door. These cars have heavy doors and I'm guessing our friend here has had these particular ones reinforced.'

They walked quietly up the paved pathway that cut through the middle of the garden, leading up to the front door. The front window was open, but the blinds were closed. As they got closer to the window, it was clear whoever was inside was interested in the news in Northern Ireland. The volume on the TV was loud enough for them to make out what was being said. The reporter was talking about a joint funeral for both the deputy first and first ministers. Laughter could be heard coming from the living room.

One of the voices finally spoke. 'Looks like we're officially ghosts.'

The other laughed and said, 'Yeah, very rich ghosts.'

Brendan recognised the voices. He looked back at Lorna. 'It's them.' He pulled his pistol from his pocket and checked the silencer was fitted.

Smith was behind him. Lorna was behind Smith with her pistol pointed into his back. Brendan placed his hand on the door handle. Pushing it down, he slowly opened the door and stepped in. The hallway had an eerie feeling to it. Without putting on the light, Brendan used the torch from his phone to go around any potential hidden obstacles. Following a dim path towards the strip of light coming from below the living room door, he led the way. Slowly approaching the door, his pistol pointed straight ahead, he came face to face with a seven-foot mahogany door.

Lorna hissed for Brendan to stop.

'What?'

'We don't know what we're walking in to.' She gestured to Smith. 'If walking in there means flying bullets, send him in first.' She pushed Smith forward. 'Move your ass.'

Brendan grabbed Smith, pulling him in front with his face almost touching the door, he ordered him to open the door and go in.

Smith's bound hands were shaking as they gripped the door handle. Lowering the handle, he pushed the door open. Light flooded out into the hallway.

'Smith? You scared the shit out of...' the voice trailed off.

From behind Smith, Brendan could see both ministers were sitting on the sofa, unarmed. He pushed Smith into the room, throwing him onto the sofa with the other two, the three lying on the sofa like rabbits caught in a trap.

'Who the hell are you?' First Minister Andrew Coleman said, his hands in the air.

'You wouldn't recognise us, we've had to change our appearance, given the fact we're wanted for your murder.' Brendan sat down on the leather seat in the corner, gun still pointed at the sofa. Lorna stood at the fireplace.

'Brendan Cleary.' Deputy First Minister Sean McManus sighed.

'And to think I voted for you.' Brendan spoke sarcastically. 'The Sinn Fein leader: a man of the people. For the people of Ireland.' He looked at the other. 'And you, Coleman – you'd have Ian Paisley turning in his grave.'

'You can talk, Cleary,' McManus replied. 'You forget what your dad was,' he looked at Coleman. Then back as Brendan. 'Your dad...'

Before he could say another word, Brendan shot the seat between the heads McManus and Coleman. 'My father taught me quite a lot, actually. Including how to fire a weapon.'

'He loves using that trick,' Smith mumbled, appearing more confident now that he wasn't by himself.

Brendan shot Smith in the foot.

Smith's cries echoed through the room. Lorna ran and closed the windows.

'And you?' Coleman turned to Smith who was rolling around on the sofa, grabbing his foot with his hands still bound. 'Why the fuck did you bring them here?' He punched Smith in the face.

'How much do you want, Brendan?' McManus asked calmly. 'We can give you a cut of the money.'

'We just want you bastards to pay for this,' Lorna finally spoke from the mantel. 'We want to see you three as well as the British and Irish prime ministers be labelled for what you all are: murderers.'

'Hughes was right, we should have gotten rid of you before this,' Smith said.

'What are you talking about. Hughes?' Brendan said. 'You had Hughes killed at the same time you planned to have us killed.'

Smith half laughed, half groaned. 'Hughes planned the trip to Belfast to get you released, Brendan. He planned the whole thing. To have your grandfather poisoned, to have Jonty start a fight with you on the day of your grandfather's funeral. He knew that if you didn't kill him, you'd do him some serious damage. Resulting in him and the lovely Lorna over here, getting you out with some bull-shit story.'

Brendan looked at Lorna. Her eyes were glazed over. A tear ran down her face as she clenched her jaw. She nodded her head. 'It's true, Brendan. I'm sorry.'

'This is what's been bothering you since we left London?' Brendan said. 'You found this out searching his office?'

'Yes. The bastard betrayed everyone.'

Brendan looked back at the three on the sofa. 'So, why'd you take him out and not all of us?'

'Our guy was supposed to take all of you out, but the incompetent piece of shit messed it up and hasn't even called in to explain what happened.'

'Can't trust anyone, can you?' Lorna laughed, without humour.

'So, what were you all planning to do? Divide the cash and sail off on a cruise ship forever?'

'Something like that,' McManus said.

'Okay, we've got you three,' Brendan looked at Lorna. 'We need to get the two prime ministers, I don't care if we have to do a televised exposure of these twats.'

'In fact, that would be a good idea,' Lorna said. 'But there's one thing bugging me, the...'

'... hit man.' Brendan finished. 'If he's still out there, he could be watching us.'

She nodded, then looked at Smith. 'Was it him you hired to do the job?'

'Who's him?' Brendan said, sounding confused.

'"The Gent" and yes, it was him we gave the job to,' Smith said.

'Who's "The Gent"?'

'He's the guy the British government hires when they need a job doing,' Lorna said. 'Which is more worrying, because he's so good you'd think he wasn't a killer. He's always cool, calm and collected. That's why he's called The Gent, because if you didn't know him, you'd think he was the nicest guy in the world.'

'Whereas in fact he's the most dangerous man the British government has at their disposal,' Smith said. 'But he fucked up this time.'

'Right,' Brendan said. 'This isn't good. If he's out there, I'm sure he's still hunting us. Guys like that don't accept failure. And it won't be long until he comes to finish the job. That's why you haven't heard from him yet,' he looked at Lorna. 'because he hasn't finished the job.'

'We need to draw him in, at the same time getting them into the public eye.' Lorna broke off and looked at the TV.

Brendan turned around. 'Turn that up,' he shouted at McManus.

BBC News was broadcasting a live feed from Belfast. The New IRA was giving a televised speech. It said that due to the attacks on the Catholic community and the murder of the Sinn Fein leader, former IRA commander, they now saw this as an act of war against the Catholic community and were recruiting new members into their ranks. They claimed membership had gone from six hundred to ten thousand strong and was growing fast.

'Jesus fucking Christ!' Lorna looked at Brendan. 'It'll only be a matter of time before there's a loyalist uprising as well.' She stormed across the room, her pistol pointed at Smith's head. 'Give me one good reason why I shouldn't just blow your head off right now.'

Brendan gently pulled her away. 'Because he's not worth it.' He kept his stare on the TV as it displayed the president of the United States pleading for calm in Belfast and Derry.

'Right, we're going to wait here. We'll get the British and Irish prime ministers to come here,' Brendan said. He looked at Lorna. 'What do you know about this hitman? One of us may need to go hunting for him.'

'Very little,' she said. She looked at Smith. 'But I'm sure he'll be happy to help.'

Smith shuffled in the seat, still grabbing his foot.

'I'll go out to the car and bring in the first aid kit,' Brendan said. 'You get him talking.'

Brendan stepped outside. He could see ice glistening on the windows as he approached the vehicle, there wasn't a cloud in the sky. He grabbed the first aid kit and slammed the door shut again. As he turned, a couple staggered past.

As he walked back up the pathway into the house, he scanned everywhere around him. The bushes, the trees, the shadows, under the cars. Brendan was tough, and fearless. But just like anyone who'd just found out one of the most sought-after contract killers was tasked with eliminating them, he couldn't help but wonder where the attack would come from. His senses sharpened.

He stepped in the front door. Closed it and locked it, leaving the key in the lock. Walking back into the sitting room, he threw the first aid kit at McManus.

'You help him.'

McManus snatched the first aid kit. 'I should let you bleed.' He pulled Smith's shoe off, followed by the sock. 'Bringing them here - what were you thinking?' He grabbed a cushion case and began wiping the blood.

'So,' Brendan said. 'Where can we find this assassin?'

'I'm looking through his file now,' Lorna said. Her eyes scanned the screen of her laptop. 'He gave me access to his file while you were out at the car.'

'Cleary, this is a professional killer,' Coleman shouted across the room. 'If you go after him, you won't win. There's a reason why he's the first person Smith calls when he needs a good job done.'

'Shut up, you fool! Let him go,' Smith shouted.

'That makes me even more curious.' Brendan sat down in front of the TV while Lorna continued to scan through the laptop. 'Why did he miss, not one, but two targets?' He paused for a moment. 'Either way, I want to pay him a visit.'

'He lives in a farmhouse just outside Gravesend,' Lorna said. 'No family - lives by himself. He has two dogs, kept in a kennel in the back garden. He's thirty-nine, likes seafood and drinks one glass of Jack Daniels before he goes to bed every night.'

'What is that, his psychiatric report?' Brendan joked.

'It's exactly that,' she replied, as she continued to scan the screen. 'He's a bit of a loner, although he does have a different woman back there after he finishes every "job" and he's a big fan of martial arts. He'll be a handful, with or without a weapon.'

'I can handle him, don't worry about that,' Brendan said, as he approached the wounded Smith. 'It's just a toe, you won't miss it.'

'Fuck you,' Smith shouted.

'You're lucky it wasn't your head.' Brendan turned and walked towards Lorna. 'What's the address. I'll go check it out.'

'Just emailed you the location.' Lorna closed the laptop and jumped up from the seat. She touched Brendan on the arm. 'Are you sure you want to go by yourself?'

'Somebody needs to stay here and watch these three clowns.' He looked at the three on the sofa. 'This stops tonight, before anyone else dies.' He looked back at Lorna. 'I'll be fine.' He pecked her on the cheek. 'I'll call you when I get there.'

'Be careful!' she shouted, as he left the room.

'Try and get your hands on those two prime ministers. Heads are going to roll tonight. The right heads this time.' He closed the door and left.

Climbing up into the Range Rover, he opened the email from Lorna and accessed the address on Google maps. Forty-five minutes estimated arrival time.

'Okay, Gent, I want a wee word with you.'

# Chapter Twenty-Seven

JUST AFTER TEN THIRTY, Brendan pulled up to a two-hundred-yard-long country driveway. He looked at the house, then drove past for another half mile. He pulled the car over and parked it on the grass verge. Checking his pistol was loaded, he jumped out and called Lorna.

'Brendan, are you okay?'

'I've just arrived. The house looks empty, but I'll have a look anyway. Any luck your end?'

'I'm looking through some files. The British prime minister is meeting the Irish prime minister at Number Ten first thing tomorrow. An emergency meeting to discuss the Northern Ireland crisis, hopeful to find a resolution, fast.'

'I'll bet they are,' Brendan said.

'I'm going to ask one of our friends to call both ministers. Tell them to get here, screw their breakfast.'

'How about we call someone in from the BBC? We can have a little live discussion on air.'

'Not a bad idea, but I don't know who we can trust. I think it's better to keep the group small.'

'Okay.' Brendan hopped over the three-foot-high wall that surrounded the grounds of The Gent's house. 'I'll call you back in a while.' He signed off.

He stayed on the grass as much as he could, not wanting the clicks of hard-heeled shoes to give him away. Even if The Gent wasn't in, he wouldn't want his two dogs going crazy.

He stepped over a flower bed onto the front entrance of recently laid brick. Sand was still in some areas. The grass had no thickness. The smell of paint still lingered in the air. This house was not of long standing.

He approached the front door, number thirty-three. He placed his hand on the black door handle and opened the door. The Gent was clearly smart enough not to keep anything incriminating inside the house. Otherwise, the house would have been locked up like a bank vault.

The hallway was empty. Not even a carpet. Each footstep sent echoes bouncing off the four walls. The living room was the same. Not even a sofa. The kitchen, empty too.

'Dead end,' he said. On his way back out of the house, blinding headlights lit up the entire room. He jumped away from the window. The sound of a car engine shutting down was followed by the headlights retreating out of the room. Darkness again. 'Okay, Gent, let's see what you're made of.'

Brendan stood behind the front door, waiting to make an introduction.

He listened as footsteps grew louder.

The door opened and in walked someone about the same height and build as Brendan. Brendan was taught never to give away his accent. This was drilled into him by his father during his training. Of course, if this guy was trained by the same people that trained Brendan's father, this was probably going to be an altercation with zero words used.

The door closed. Brendan went to floor Gent with a blow to the back of the head, but the man ducked and spun around, catching Brendan's second blow. He was fast. After two failed attempts to floor The Gent, Brendan knew this wasn't going to be a walk in the park.

Gent was wearing a trench coat and leather gloves. In the dark, Brendan couldn't make out his face. He could see the dark outline and that was it. Gent grabbed Brendan, Brendan head butted him. Gent stumbled back, but before Brendan could capitalise, Gent rugby tackled Brendan, running him into the wall. Brendan drove his elbow into his back and kneed him in the head sending him down to the ground. As Brendan went to kick him, he rolled away, springing back to his feet. This time Gent produced a flick knife. The seven-inch blade came towards Brendan's mid-section. He grabbed Gent's wrist, trying to reverse the momentum, then Gent sunk his forehead into Brendan's nose. Brendan stumbled back and before he could recover, Gent's foot flew up and caught him on the temple. As he fell, he cracked his head on the radiator and passed out.

Some moments later he woke to the sound of his phone ringing. It was Lorna.

'Brendan, why haven't you answered your phone?'

'I just met The Gent.' He sat up groggily, with his back against the wall. 'He's one tough bastard.'

'I told you he was dangerous. Are you okay?'

'I'm alive, which doesn't make sense. Why didn't he kill me?'

'Don't question your good fortune. Just come back. You need to see the news. We're officially dead.'

'Okay.' Brendan pushed himself into the wall, using it to bring himself back up to his feet. 'This should be fun.'

THE GENT'S CAR WAS gone. Brendan had blown his chance of catching the man contracted to take him and Lorna out. But none of it made sense. Who was Gent working for? The most highly-skilled assassin used by the British government didn't miss his mark. And leaving his target unconscious in his house was not how it should be.

He got back into the Range Rover and immediately put the heating on. Reversing the Google maps directions, he began the return journey. The sting in his hand as he gripped the steering wheel reminded him that he had gripped the assassin's knife, but he forced the pain to the back of his mind.

Driving through the quiet streets of suburban London, he decided to entertain himself with the growing fictional story that was now his and Lorna's lives. He was amused at the fact he was supposed to be dead. In that moment, an idea flashed across his mind. How free would he be if he stayed dead? He knew his life would never be the same again anyway. Especially in Belfast. He could never walk down the streets. And he didn't want to go back to the life he had in Belfast, anyway.

On the radio show, there was a debate about what had happened at Stormont. From the BBC's Belfast station, an emergency debate was held. The heads of the four leading political parties were dragged in to provide what they were elected for: leadership. It was so unexpected. So fast. Unbelievable. The whole thing was almost laughable. But the knife wound on Brendan's hand proved it was no laughing matter.

During the debate, the reporter cut to a live feed from the Shankill Road where fifteen houses had been petrol bombed. The Orange Hall at the bottom of the Shankill Road had gone up in flames and two local residents who'd tried to stop the perpetrators doing it had been shot dead. David Allen – vice president of the DUP could be heard standing up in the news room and throwing his bottle of water across the studio. Aine McPeake of Sinn Fein could be heard shouting at Allen, followed by an uproar in the group of politicians.

The Police Service of Northern Ireland had stretched their resources to the brink and were asking for assistance from Britain and the Republic of Ireland to help prevent a bloodbath on the streets.

'Hopefully they won't need to...' Brendan switched stations, tired of listening to the bullshit that only he and Lorna knew wasn't true. And until the Irish people – both Catholic and Protestant – knew it was not true, a lot of people were going to get hurt. He chose a station of relaxing music. A programme called "End of the Day Relax" which couldn't be further away from what he usually listened to. But one thing that brought him home to his childhood training was his dad playing this weird music. His father used to make him sit cross-legged with his eyes closed for what seemed like an eternity. Until that moment in the car, he never knew what every individual piece of training his dad put him through, meant.

He pulled up to the safe house just as his phone rang. It was Lorna.

'I've just pulled up, but I'm not sure if I can go into a house that's haunted with ghosts.' He heard Lorna laugh. 'I'm glad this hasn't ruined your sense of humour.'

As he stepped inside, his sense of smell was assaulted. The house reeked of cigarette smoke. He entered the sitting room into a haze of smoke.

'Wouldn't let them go without a smoke.' Lorna said, sitting at the writing bureau in the corner of the room, looking bored. She looked at Brendan's hand. 'So, you had a dance with The Gent? Looks like you put up a good fight.'

'Why didn't he kill you, the piece of shit?' Smith shouted across the room. 'The son of a bitch has turned on us.'

'Looks like you'll have to bring in number two from now on,' Lorna said. 'Or has he already been promoted to number one?'

'Fuck you,' Smith shouted.

She looked at Brendan. 'I've tried to get in touch with the two ministers, but there is no response from either of them.'

'Probably window shopping,' Brendan joked. He snatched the first aid box from Smith. Squirting some antiseptic into his wound, he gritted his teeth. His eyes watered. Wrapping his hand with a dressing he made a fist. 'Don't try and grab the blade from an assassin who's trying to jab it into your stomach, or you'll end up with a cut that hurts like hell.'

The captives didn't respond. They just carried on watching the late-night extended news programme of people on the streets of Belfast and Derry trying to protect their neighbourhoods.

'Forty years ago it was understandable for people to do this ... not today,' Lorna said.

'They probably would have said that back then, too,' Brendan replied. 'The truth is, they've been attacked. Now they want to protect themselves. Doesn't matter if it's today, forty years, or one hundred years ago. Fear is fear. People protect themselves when they fear their lives are threatened.'

'Greed is greed, too,' Lorna said. 'The only difference is that forty years ago, the Irish prime minister lost his nerve. This time, that hasn't happened.'

Smith's phone sounded. It was the prime minister. Brendan ordered him to answer it and play it cool.

'Yes, Sir.' Smith paused, looking around the room. 'Yes, Sir...I've been trying to call. You need to get to the safe house. We've had a problem.' He paused again. The rest of the room could just about hear the prime minister's voice coming through the phone. 'Sir,' Smith's tone sounded like he was addressing an equal now and not the prime minister. 'With all due respect, what your wife will think about you leaving at this time is not important. What is important, is that you get your ass here – now, Sir.' Smith stopped again. 'Yes, Sir.' He hung up. 'He's on his way.'

'We wouldn't want the poor old prime minister to get into trouble with the good wife now, would we,' Brendan said. He sat down beside Lorna. 'How about we compile all the evidence we've got. Keep it all together?'

'Already done,' Lorna said. 'Copies have been emailed to ten different email accounts.' She looked over at the three captives. 'Just in case something happens us.'

# Chapter Twenty-Eight

THE TIME WAS A QUARTER to midnight and still no sign of the prime minister. Brendan sat on the ground, with his back against the door, his arms resting on his raised knees. Waiting patiently for Thorn to arrive, he kept his eyes on the others the entire time. Twirling his pistol in his index finger.

'You better be careful you don't accidently shoot someone. That's not a toy, son!' Coleman shouted.

Brendan fired a shot, missing Coleman's head by no more than an inch. The plaster that flew off the wall didn't miss his head, showering him. 'Don't call me son.'

'We should call you Billy the Kid,' Lorna joked.

Brendan checked his phone. BBC News said there was an update to the ongoing civil crisis in Belfast. The British prime minister had changed his plans and instead of having the Irish prime minister come to London, he was now due to meet with his Irish counterpart first thing in the morning at Stormont. Toner was spending the night in Belfast and would greet Thorn when he arrived.

'At least we now know where Toner is.' Brendan jumped up and grabbed the remote control for the TV. He put on the news channel broadcasting live from Stormont. The Irish prime minister was speaking to the camera to say he was in Belfast to assure the people of the city that they had his full support.

Brendan looked at Lorna. 'How about returning to the scene of the crime?'

She looked at him, not sure what he meant or where he was going with it.

Before Brendan could say another word, Smith's phone went off. Brendan grabbed it. It was Thorn. Brendan answered the call and put the phone to Smith's ear.

'Yes, Sir?' Smith looked up at Brendan. 'Yes, Sir. I'll get the door.'

Brendan hung up the phone. He looked at Lorna then left the room. Walking across the hallway, he stopped behind the door ready to switch on the light. He could hear the clicks of a pair of hard-heeled shoes getting closer to the door. He pulled the door open before Thorn had a chance to knock.

'Who in God's name are you?'

'Apparently, Prime Minister, I'm a ghost.'

The prime minister looked hard at Brendan, scanning every inch of his face. 'Cleary?'

Brendan produced his pistol from behind the door. 'Get in.'

Thorn reluctantly put one foot in the doorway and stopped. He looked back to where his car was parked. Brendan grabbed him by the knot of his tie and dragged him into the house, making sure to shut and lock the door. He ordered the VIP to make his way towards the living room.

Acting cool as a cucumber, Thorn strolled into the sitting room, hands in the pockets of his overcoat. He looked at Lorna, then spun on his heel towards the sofa. He sighed and dropped his head. 'I knew you were an incompetent fool.' He glared at Smith as Brendan followed him into the room and shut the door.

'Don't get too comfortable, Prime Minister,' Brendan said. 'We've got a flight to catch.' He looked at Lorna. 'I think it'll be a nice surprise for the Irish prime minister when, in front of all those camera's he's greeted by all of us, not just him. What do you think?'

Lorna looked surprised - excited. 'Let's go.'

'Hold on a minute,' the prime minister said. 'How do you possibly expect to get us all to Stormont,' he laughed. 'Come on Cleary, you can't...'

'You are the prime minister. And we're all going to accompany you in the ministerial vehicle until we reach RAF Northolt. From there we'll be flying to Stormont. Lorna and I will be stepping out of the chopper to greet the Irish prime minister while the world sees how much shit you've all cooked up.'

'Don't insult our intelligence by trying to deny it either,' Lorna said. 'I've emailed evidence to ten different people in the intelligence world. One of them is an old friend in the CIA.' She stood up and grabbed her bag, throwing a set of handcuffs at the prime minister. 'You know what to do.'

Thorn put the cuffs on. 'I need to make a call to my wife, I need to tell her...'

'You can call your wife when you're in custody tomorrow,' Lorna said. 'Let's go, this house gives me the creeps.'

Lorna led the way out the door. Brendan went last. They all stepped out into the cool night. Walking towards the ministerial vehicle, Brendan looked at the Jaguar XJ.

'This isn't going to work. The car's too small,' Thorn said.

'Okay, which one of you four wants to go in the boot?'

Lorna laughed. 'You can't be serious.'

Brendan tapped on the boot. 'Deadly serious.' None of them answered. Brendan opened the boot. Smith was closest to him. Grabbing him, he dragged him over to the boot. 'In you get. You'll be alright, it'll only be for an hour and a half.'

'The rest of you get in the car,' Lorna said. 'You want to drive or will I?'

'I'll sit in the back with Coleman and the prime minister. McManus, you can be co-pilot.'

They all got in.

As Lorna took off, Brendan continued to check the news in Belfast. It was currently a 24-hour programme watching live from the streets. Police were everywhere. People were on the streets. Taxi depots and bus services had been cancelled through high risk zones. Two buses were hijacked on the Falls Road and were used to erect road blocks.

'It's like going back in time,' Brendan said. 'So, Prime Minister, how much were you to benefit from a fabricated referendum and a united Ireland?'

'Piss off.' Thorn's words spoke with venom.

The car fell silent. Brendan sat with his pistol gripped tightly in his hand. Lorna drove casually, just as if she was driving to the supermarket. Thorn and Coleman squirmed restlessly in their seat. McManus was taking it all in his stride. The thought of prison didn't appear to bother him. But then he had spent twelve years inside for possession of weapons and explosives during a riot in Derry and was only released after the Good Friday Agreement.

At twenty minutes to two, they pulled up to the gates of RAF Northolt. The prime minister waved to the security guard. The barrier went up without question.

'Do you know your way around here?' Brendan asked Lorna.

She nodded her head. 'This is where I came for my pilot training. I learned how to fly RAF choppers here in a previous life, before I was recruited into intelligence.'

'I guess Hughes liked that sweet ass of yours,' the prime minister said.

'I can't believe I voted for you.'

'It wouldn't surprise me if that election was rigged, too,' Brendan sniggered.

'You'd be surprised how many countries around the world have bought their way into power.' Thorn sounded as if he was trying to justify his actions.

'But how many were happy to sacrifice so many innocent people to get their way?' Lorna asked.

'Aw, come now, Agent Woodward. The Irish people aren't worth worrying about. They do nothing but fight anyway. They bring it on themselves. They're even known for being a fighting nation – even though they can't seem to win a war without someone's help. They're nothing but a bunch of peasants.' Thorn spoke with an overly posh accent. 'The British people would be much better off not carrying that pathetic nation. They're not of the same class as us, Lorna. Not sophisticated like us. Like you and me.'

'You shut the fuck up,' McManus screamed from the front seat.

'Let him talk,' Brendan said. 'It'll give him practice for all the talking he needs to do in front of the news cameras in the morning.'

Lorna pulled up to the chopper. 'Let's go.' She got out of the car. 'Can't forget Smith.' She reached into the car and pressed the boot release on the inside of the driver's door.

Brendan got out and dragged Coleman behind him.

The prime minister got out of the other side. Still with his smugness, he strolled around with his hands in his pockets. He was too cool. Not acting like Smith, a blubbering baby crying his eyes out.

Lorna jumped into the pilot's seat.

'Where are you taking us? This thing won't get us to Belfast. It's over four hundred miles away.'

Lorna nodded. 'It'll get us to RAF Brize Norton. There, we can use the ministerial jet.'

Before the aircraft took off, Brendan made sure the other four were strapped in and bound to their seats. 'Prime Minister Thorn, I trust you've already arranged for your flight crew to have you in Belfast for your nine o'clock meeting with the Irish prime minister?'

Thorn nodded.

'Good. Let's go.'

# Chapter Twenty-Nine

AFTER A FORTY-MINUTE flight, Lorna impressed all the passengers by landing the aircraft within a few hundred yards of the jet they'd be taking across the Irish sea to Belfast.

The prime minister's crew were already there waiting. Two RAF pilots had Thorn Force One ready to take off. Two flight attendants waited at the bottom of the steps that led up to the cabin.

Brendan told Lorna to keep her pistol on the four captives. He got out first, produced his pistol and ordered the four out. Lorna was last to exit. Both Brendan and Lorna kept their pistols pointed as they walked across the open runway.

As they got to the steps of Thorn Force One, the prime minister approached the two flight attendants who thought it was all a joke. 'Don't panic, ladies. Just get into the plane.'

'Not so fast,' Brendan said. 'Nobody's going anywhere until we know who's on that jet.' He looked at Lorna. 'Do you want to check it out, or will I?'

'I'll do it.' Lorna made her way up the steps, disappearing into the aircraft.

Brendan kept his pistol on the growing number of hostages. The flight attendants looked both shocked and scared. They looked at Coleman and McManus.

'Yes, they're dead,' Brendan said. 'So am I, apparently.'

The flight attendants looked like they'd been newly recruited into the RAF. They certainly didn't appear confident in dealing with the situation they found themselves. But then again, how often did something like this happen?

'Don't worry, you won't be harmed,' Brendan reassured them. 'If it's any consolation, I'm sorry you've been dragged into this.'

Lorna shouted down from the cabin. 'Everything's clear in here. I've locked the pilots in their cabin. Let's go.'

'You heard her.' Brendan pushed his pistol into the back of Smith. Smith went first, followed by Thorn, then McManus and Coleman. Finally, Brendan followed the two flight attendants up the steps. Half way up the steps, he heard a crack in the distance. A gunshot. Before he could react, a force pushed him from his right side, then the reality kicked in. And pain arrived. He'd been shot. He scrambled back up to his feet. The shooter was smart enough to shoot the side that was holding the gun. Brendan stood back up to see his own gun pointed at his face. One of the flight attendants, a tall blonde-haired lady who looked no more than early twenties stood, holding his Glock with both hands. The barrel trembling right in front of his eyes.

'Don't make me shoot you, Sir.' Her name badge said Lisa. She spoke with a Northern English accent that trembled in sync with her hands. Brendan stood gripping his shoulder. He knew Lisa didn't want to shoot him, but her job and training would have expected it. 'Please, make your way back to the ground. I can't let this plane go anywhere under a hostage situation.'

Brendan turned and walked back down the steps, his eyes scanning the area for the shooter. 'Lisa, right? You realise the government you've signed up to work for has told lies about what's going on in Belfast?'

'We can talk about it when you're in custody.'

'For God's sake, Lisa. I'm supposed to be dead. The two Irish ministers that I've just got onto the plane are supposed to be dead. And the lies came from Thorn. We're flying to Belfast to clear my name and the name of my colleague.' He looked up at the steps to see Lorna held at gunpoint by Thorn.

Brendan dropped his head and shook it. He looked up at Lisa who still had the pistol pointed at him. 'Lisa, come on. Do you really want to be responsible for innocent deaths?' He looked up the steps of the jet as the prime minister disembarked with a smug grin on his face, McManus, Coleman and Smith with him. 'Come on, Lisa, help us.'

'If you're innocent, then it will all be revealed when we get you into custody.' Her eyes glazed as a vehicle's headlights approached from behind Brendan. He turned to see an RAF regiment jeep approach.

'Come on, Lisa. Do you think they're going to let us live? They can't afford to.'

Lisa didn't know where to look. Brendan could tell she was changing her mind as she looked at the prime minister disembark the aircraft, grinning as he pressed the gun into Lorna's back. Brendan turned and watched two RAF personnel jump from their vehicle. He looked at Lorna. She was looking at him, speechless.

'Well done, Miss.' Thorn handed his pistol to Coleman and took Lisa's. 'I'm afraid none of you can go anywhere.'

The two RAF personnel slowly approached the group, their L85 rifles raised, resting on their shoulders.

Thorn was happy to see them. 'Boy, am I glad to see you two.' He walked towards them. 'Please, lower your weapons. Everything's under control.'

They both did as instructed.

'Sir, what's going on here?' One of the two asked.

'Part of the SA80 family, correct?' Thorn took the man's gun. Inspecting it closely, he looked at McManus. 'What do you think of this?'

McManus took the rifle. The prime minister took the other. 'I do like these weapons.' He saluted the two. 'What are your names?'

The taller of the two was thin with a chiselled face. He straightened himself up and saluted Thorn. 'Lance Corporal Williams, Sir.'

'At ease,' Thorn said. He shook Williams' hand. 'And you, young man?'

The other was a few inches shorter than Thorn's five-foot ten height and was built like a rugby player. He was black and spoke with a Liverpool accent. 'Corporal Hogg, Sir.'

'At ease, Corporal. Good work.' Thorn patted Hogg on the shoulder and walked around the two in a circle as if he was their commanding officer inspecting their appearance.

'We've got to go,' Smith shouted.

'Nigel, we've been seen, you stupid bastard!' Coleman shouted. 'We can't let any of them go free.'

'I'm not stupid,' Thorn shouted. 'Smith, go and alert the pilots that we're leaving.'

'Excuse me, Sir,' Lisa said. 'I think we should wait until...'

Thorn turned, raised the rifle and shot Lisa in the head. Her body hit the ground right at Brendan's feet. Lorna jumped in shock, covering her mouth with the palm of her hand.

Thorn turned and told the Corporal and Lance Corporal to cuff Brendan and Lorna. 'Brendan, why did you have to shoot Lisa.' He grinned at McManus.

McManus shook his head. 'You're fucking sick.'

'What? I didn't shoot her, Brendan did. Just like he did everyone else.' He looked at Brendan, then stroked Lorna's face. 'At least that's what the police are going to think. I'll be a hero for catching them.' He raised the gun. Put it to Lorna's head. 'Why did you have to kill the beautiful Agent Woodward and these young members of Her Majesty's forces?'

'Fuck you,' Lorna shouted.

'Fine, have it your...' The side of Thorn's face exploded in blood, he dropped the gun and fell to his knees, screaming and holding the side of his head. A second shot rang out, followed by a third. McManus screamed. The rifle had been shot, but he was spared. Brendan lunged and grabbed the gun McManus dropped. Lorna got her hands on the one Thorn had to her head.

Brendan looked at the two RAF men. 'We've got to get out of here.' He looked at Lisa's corpse. 'Get her body out of here. She deserves a bit of dignity.' He kicked Thorn in the side, looking all around, expecting another bullet. 'Get your ass up and get in that plane now.'

'Fuck you,' Thorn shouted. 'Shoot me.'

'Come on,' Williams shouted to Hogg to help him. The two dragged Thorn to his feet. 'What do you want done with him?'

Brendan looked all around the airfield. Where's the sniper?

'Get him on the plane,' Lorna shouted. 'He's got a meeting with the Irish prime minister at nine, sharp.' She too, was looking around the airfield. 'Do you believe in guardian angels?'

'I'm starting to,' Brendan said.

'How's your shoulder?'

'I'll live. At least until we see this through.'

They were climbing the steps of the aircraft, grateful to see the inside of the cabin, when a voice from Brendan's past – one that couldn't possibly be there, sounded – and was proof that ghosts do exist.

'Brendan. Wait.'

Brendan froze in his tracks. He looked at Lorna. Her jaw had almost hit the ground.

'Wait, son. I'm coming with you.'

Brendan turned and looked down the flight of steps. Were his eyes deceiving him? Was that really his father looking up at him? The hairs on the back of his neck stood up. Seven years worth of questions flooded his mind. He blinked. His father was still there, now climbing the steps of Thorn Force One. Cradling an L115A3 rifle.

'There's no time to chat. I'll explain everything on the way. Let's go.

# Chapter Thirty

FLYING OVER THE IRISH sea, Belfast bound, there was an awkward silence. Lance Corporal Williams had stopped the bleeding on Brendan's shoulder. Prime Minister Thorn was having his wound attended to by Hogg, not that there was much left of his ear. Brendan looked at the prime minister's grimace with a healthy dose of humour.

'Good shot,' Lorna said to Damien Cleary as she gestured towards Thorn. 'Or were you aiming for the head?'

Damien laughed. 'Guess we'll never know.'

'Enough of the small talk, bollocks,' Brendan shouted, pulling a grimace of his own as Williams poured some alcohol on the wound. 'Where the fuck have you been. We all thought you were dead.'

'Obviously not,' Smith smirked.

Damien stomped on Smiths foot where it had been shot earlier.

'I had to disappear, Brendan.' Damien gestured at Thorn. 'I had become a target by so many. I'm talking about all over the world.' He stood up. 'The Russians, South Americans, the Chinese, the Italian mafia – I'd been involved with each of these groups. They had to think I was dead or they'd have come after me. And if they couldn't find me, they'd have hurt you and your mother to get to me.'

'You could have taken us with you.'

'You wouldn't have wanted to live a life of always looking over your shoulder, son.'

'What about mum? You know she drank herself to death? The thought of you lying in some ditch drove her into an early grave.'

'He became too good.' Thorn laughed from his seat. 'The more he did for our government, the more valuable he became.'

'Not only valuable,' Smith mumbled, still in pain. 'But a liability. The amount of information you have on some of the most powerful...'

'Most corrupt you mean.' Damien corrected him.

'...governments around the world. You'd have enough to start World War Three.'

'You were simply in too deep, Damien, my good man,' Thorn said.

Damien turned his attention back to his son. 'It all started in Belfast. They wanted someone to bring down both organisations. And shortly after they recruited me, their incompetent international spies either didn't have the balls or just didn't have the ability to do their jobs. Therefore, I became...'

'Our secret weapon,' Smith said. 'Our number one go-to guy to fix any problems we were faced with. Before we had The Gent, we had Damien Cleary.'

'You won't be seeing The Gent again, he's dead,' Damien said.

They all looked at him.

Damien looked at Brendan. 'You want to know why The Gent didn't shoot you and Lorna at the Orange Hall when Hughes was taken out? Because it was...'

'It was you?' Lorna's breathing deepening. 'How did you know?'

'I knew The Gent was contracted to take out you, Brendan and Hughes. That was going to be used to create a story to say you were all involved in something dirty.'

'So, *you* took out our number one killer?' Thorn asked. Then he laughed. 'Well, doesn't surprise me. You were always of a different calibre. Brendan, Damien, listen. Why don't we all cut a deal here. I can make both of you very comfortable for the rest of your lives.'

'You're lucky you're still breathing.' Lorna jumped up from her seat. Grabbing Thorn by the throat, she thrust her face into his. 'You're in no position to bargain.'

'Have either of you two thought about what you're doing when we get to Belfast?' Damien stood up as if he was ready to start directing them. 'We want as many eyes to see them two tits as possible.' He gestured at Coleman and McManus.

'I've got a friend in the CIA using their connections to have global eyes on Stormont when we arrive,' Lorna said. 'They've been emailed all the documents we've gathered.'

Thorn lost his smug grin. The realisation that he wasn't going to worm his way out of this was starting to hit home.

'What about you?' Brendan looked at his dad. 'You show your face again and the world will know you're alive.' He stood up to look his father in the eye.

They were almost identical. It was as if Damien was looking at a thirty-seven-year-old hologram. 'I came alive again because I knew you were in trouble, son. I'm not leaving you now. We can clear your name and Lorna's. After that we'll figure out what we're going to do. I've got the resources to make us all disappear for the rest of our lives.'

'Ten minutes until we reach Aldergrove!' Lorna shouted from the door of the cockpit. 'We need transportation into Belfast.'

Lance Corporal Williams stood up. 'We should be able to get our hands on a chopper. Under the circumstances, with the company we're keeping, it shouldn't be a problem. I know the guys based in Aldergrove.'

'The Irish prime minister is going to get a nice surprise when he sees us lot coming.' Brendan sat back down and looked out the window. The runway lights of Belfast International Airport were visible in the distance.

Ten minutes later, they touched down. The landing was smooth. The airport was almost asleep, with only the graveyard shift keeping the facilities ticking over until the morning shift arrived. The body bag with flight attendant Lisa's corpse lay across the floor, a stark reminder of the cruelty of one of the most influential men in the world.

'Our friends in the CIA have arranged for us to get to Stormont,' Lorna said, looking at her phone. She looked at Brendan with red-rimmed, glazed eyes. Brendan grabbed her hand. 'Let's go, we're nearly finished.' He looked at his father. Feeling awkward about the situation, he forced a smile. 'It's good to see you, Dad.' He reached his hand out to shake Damien's hand.

Damien pulled Brendan in for a hug.

'Aw, I'm touched,' Thorn said.

'Get your ass up.' Williams dragged Thorn off his seat. 'You're in a lot of trouble, Sir. I think it would be in your best interest to keep your mouth shut.'

'You're the boss,' Thorn spoke sarcastically, as he was pushed up to the front of the aircraft.

'Dad, go and ask the pilots if they have a spare uniform you can wear. Even if the Americans are helping us, you can't be seen.'

Brendan looked out the window. The runway crew were lining the steps up to the side of the aircraft. There were a number of RAF personnel waiting to greet the prime minister. Brendan and Lorna lined everyone up, ready to leave. Outside, it was raining.

As the door opened, Williams and Hogg both saluted the welcoming party. They asked to speak to the commanding officer on shift. Brendan and Lorna both looked at each other. Their future and their chance of getting to Stormont was currently in the hands of the RAF. All they had at that moment was faith in the good guys and their ability to believe such a story.

The commanding officer entered the aircraft, accompanied by two guards. He took his hat off and looked around the cabin at everyone. He looked down at the body bag, then looked at Thorn. The prime minister tried to say something but was floored before he could utter a word.

'Get this piece of shit off my base.'

Damien appeared, dressed as a pilot. He grabbed the prime minster and dragged him out of the plane, followed by all the rest. Brendan was the last to leave. Stepping out into the Irish drizzle, he was glad to see an RAF chopper fire up its engine.

'TV crews from the BBC, CNN and Sky News are all waiting for us to arrive at Stormont,' Lorna said. 'But I feel something in the pit of my stomach, Brendan. Something's not right. This is all too easy.'

Brendan stood at the top of the steps, ready to disembark. Looking down at the prime minister and the two – supposedly dead - ministers and of course, his father. He grabbed Lorna's hand. 'Come on, let's see how this is going to play out. If you trust your friend in the CIA then we must have some help.'

She held Brendan by the hand as they disembarked. The rain got heavier as they made their way towards the chopper. Damien looked back to make sure they were coming.

As they reached the chopper, their last journey to Stormont where they'd step out in front of the world's news cameras, Brendan and Lorna looked at each other before stepping in.

'What are you waiting for?' Damien shouted.

Brendan nudged Lorna. 'Let's go and clear our names.'

Lorna stepped into the chopper. Brendan put one foot in and was stopped by the RAF base commanding officer.

He placed his hand on Brendan's shoulder. 'I always knew he was a slimy bastard. Good luck.'

Brendan looked back at Thorn Force One, the body bag being carried down the steps. 'I can't wait to see the expression on Toner's face.'

He stepped into the chopper and it took off.

The time was seven thirty-five. The rain had past, leaving the sunrise to light up the sky in a spectacular mix of pink, yellow and blue. In the chopper, Brendan sat beside Lorna. She was staring at her phone, biting her nails, her right foot tapping. Brendan craned his head closer to see the screen of her phone. She was reading a text from Hughes.

'He's dead, Lorna. We're not.'

She closed the message and locked her phone screen. 'He was a lying bastard.' She looked at Damien, an expression of gratitude written across her face.

Damien was staring at Thorn. He looked as if everything he had taught Brendan about being smart was about to go out the window of the chopper, with Thorn going after it. He met Lorna's gaze. 'I'm not getting out of this chopper. You two will need to get out of Belfast before anyone can get their hands on you.' He glanced at Brendan, then back at Lorna. 'You may clear your names today, but do not let them take you into custody.' He looked down at Lorna's phone which had started ringing. 'Both of you understand? Make sure the world can see these bastards getting dropped off. Say a few words to the cameras. but do not let them take you in.' He looked out the window as Stormont came into view.

Lorna looked at her phone. The call came from a Daryl Zip.

'Who's that?' Brendan looked down at the screen as it continued to ring.

Lorna answered it. 'Zip's our friend in the CIA.' She put the phone to her ear.

'Can we trust him?' Brendan sounded unsure.

Lorna nodded. 'Zip, we're almost there. Okay, thank you.' She hung up. 'Well, we're all on TV. As we speak, the camera crews on the ground are filming the chopper as it approaches.' She took a deep breath, looking over at Smith, then Thorn. 'You all ready?'

The chopper began its descent, landing in the gardens of Stormont Estate. The security hut wreckage acted as a reminder of the well-planned diversion that caused the world to take its eyes off Coleman and McManus, allowing them to fake being shot.

Fifty yards from the chopper sat a grey Vauxhall Insignia. Irish Prime Minister Toner stepped out of the back. He stood up straight, buttoned his jacket closed and walked towards the chopper.

Brendan looked at Lorna. He grabbed her hand. 'Let's see his expression. You want to video it? Something for us to laugh at?'

'Brendan...' Her voice shook.

'Hey,' he squeezed her hand. 'We're going to be okay.'

The chopper's propellers shut down. Damien got Thorn to his feet, then lined up Smith, followed by McManus and Coleman ready to open the door. Camera crews were everywhere. Damien handed his phone to Brendan. 'You're about to be on the TV.'

Brendan looked at the phone. BBC news was showing live feed of the chopper. Damien thanked the RAF personnel for their help but ordered them off the chopper for their own safety. Damien then took the pilot's seat. Brendan grabbed Thorn by the back of the neck, his pistol pressed into his gut. Lorna did the same with Smith. Williams had his gun on Coleman, and Hogg did the same with McManus.

'Brendan, the second we open that door, bullets could start flying!' His dad shouted. 'Don't fuck about. We don't know who's out there.'

'I want to look Toner in the eye,' Brendan said as the Irish prime minister arrived at the bottom of the chopper's steps. 'Right, this is it, Dad, I'll be back in one second.' He slid the door open. The morning light flooded into the cabin. Toner's smile dropped into a frown. First his expression moved into one of those awkward smiles as he tried to piece together the information that was being sent to his brain from his eyes. A split second and he knew what was going on. He slowly backed away. Brendan stepped out with Thorn by the scruff of the neck. Lorna followed with Smith. Coleman and McManus were now revealed to the world.

The distant mumbles from news reporters got louder and faster as they slowly realised what was taking place. Brendan pointed his gun at Toner, shouting for him to stop where he was. Estate security swarmed the grass. A semi-circle of armed guards now had their weapons pointed at Brendan and Lorna. Damien fired the chopper's engine back up again. The propellers began to spin.

'Brendan, you've done it. Get your ass back in the chopp...'

The sound of glass being shattered from behind Brendan and Lorna caused them to spin around. Brendan turned and saw blood, splattered all over the window of the pilot's cabin. 'Dad!' he shouted. He sent a side kick into Thorn's shin, snapping it and ran back towards the chopper. Lorna followed him. Gun shots rang out, bits of grass flying into the air as ground security shouted for Brendan and Lorna to stop.

They both jumped into the chopper. Brendan frantically forced his way into the cabin. His dad was clutching his neck. Brendan grabbed Damien's hand, pulling it off his neck caused blood to spurt. 'Jesus fucking Christ, Dad!' Brendan shouted as another bullet flew in the window, hitting his father on the shoulder.

'Brendan, get him the out of that seat, now!' Lorna shouted. 'Move, we've got to get out of here! Quick.'

Brendan released his dad's seatbelt and dragged him off the seat into the back. Lorna took his place, shutting the window. She took the chopper into the air.

'Who the fuck was that?' Brendan shouted as he lay his bleeding father down on the floor of the chopper.

'I have no idea, but whoever it was didn't want this thing to get off the ground!' Lorna shouted.

Damien started coughing blood, choking. Brendan used his sleeve to wipe the blood away. He started panting, then coughing, spitting blood everywhere. He tried to speak, but blood was blocking his airway. Brendan looked into his dad's eyes, but the life was slowly fading out of them. 'I'm proud of you, son,' he whispered.

'Don't start talking that bollocks, you're going to be alright.'

'Where are we going?' Lorna shouted.

Brendan looked at his dad's neck. He was losing too much blood. He was dying. At least this time he would die in his son's arms. Knowing his father and knowing where he'd want to go to die he shouted, 'get us to Donegal!'

His dad couldn't speak, but he nodded his head and smiled, his eyes rolling in the back of his head. Brendan had made the right decision.

'I love you, Dad.' Brendan's eyes filled with water. Covered in his father's blood, he could do nothing more than hold him.

# Chapter Thirty-One

SITTING IN ESTATE'S gardens looking out to sea, Brendan didn't blink. His face had as much life as a statue. Each wave coming in from the Atlantic brought with it another reminder of the holidays he had spent here with the man who was laid out on the grass only five feet away from where he sat.

Lorna approached him from behind. Placing her hand on his shoulder, she kissed him on the cheek. 'I'm not going to ask if you are okay.' She sat down beside him. 'For what it's worth, our names have been cleared. We're all over the news. The documents – all the evidence we gathered on the British and Irish governments - have landed in the right hands.' She poured two cups of coffee and handed one to Brendan, but he refused it. 'Our friends in the CIA pulled through. I knew there had to be someone out there on our side.' She took a sip of her coffee. 'So, what are we going...'

'We find out who the shooter is.' He looked at the dead body of his father, then back at Lorna. 'Well, I'm going to find out.' He grabbed Lorna's hand. 'You're free to go and do what you want. You've got your life back.'

She looked at him, her eyes tiny slits, puckering her lips. 'What? And let you have all the fun?' She stroked his face. 'We're in this together. You're not getting rid of me, Brendan Cleary.' She looked around at the body of his father. 'He once said that all the training the British government put him through would come back to haunt them.' She finished her coffee then looked at Brendan. 'Looks like he was right.'

Brendan forced a smile, looking at his father. 'I'm just getting started...'

*HI GUYS. IF YOU ENJOYED this book, I would be extremely grateful if you could leave me a brief review. Reviews help my author career which I'm very passionate about growing. Especially being a new author, reviews are something that really help me and others like me. If you'd like to help, you can access the book's review page by clicking the following links. Just click on the link from the store you shopped from:*

UK STORE[1]

US STORE[2]

**FREE BOOK!** Visit P.M. Heron's website by clicking here[3] and sign up to receive a FREE book, information about conventions, special offers and other titles in this series and other

1. https://www.amazon.co.uk/Bloody-Thursday-Brendan-Cleary-Novel-ebook/dp/B07GYY1FTX/ref=pd_rhf_ee_p_img_1?_encoding=UTF8&psc=1&refRID=EKM3CTVA1AP37Z3J8RK8
2. https://www.amazon.com/Bloody-Thursday-Brendan-Cleary-Novel-ebook/dp/B07GYY1FTX/ref=sr_1_1?ie=UTF8&qid=1536452278&sr=8-1&keywords=dexter+bradgate&dpID=41oGFYUErTL&preST=_SY445_QL70_&dpSrc=srch
3. http://pmheronauthor.com/

series. In the following pages you'll find the first two chapters of the book following Bloody Thursday: *BEST SERVED COLD*

# Chapter One

LAKE COMO: SITUATED on the foothills on the Alps, close to the border between Italy and Switzerland. Little more than one thousand miles in distance from Belfast. But for Brendan Cleary: another world.

Brendan woke to see the oval window's silk drapes blowing high in the air. The cool air hit his shirtless torso reminding him that even in places like Italy, it was still cold at this time of the year. November in Italy wasn't as cold as Ireland, but it wasn't warm enough to sleep without a heavy duvet.

He got up off the bed and trudged across the room, his eyesight slowly coming into focus.

'What are you doing?' Lorna groaned, as he slammed the window shut. 'What time is it?'

'Not time to get up yet,' he said. 'Just stopping the draft. It's freezing.' He jogged back across the room and climbed into the bed. Instantly feeling the warmth tingling all over his body. He lay on his back, one hand behind his head and the other gripping his shoulder where he'd been shot. The wound had long healed, but it was still tender.

Lorna rolled over towards him, laying her head on his chest. 'Are you okay?'

'What do you mean?'

'I heard you crying in your sleep.'

'Was I...'

'Calling for him, again?' She nodded her head.

'It'll pass.' He tried to shrug it off as nothing. 'I had nightmares for years about him when I thought he was dead the first time.'

'Yes, but this time...'

'I'm all right, Lorna,' he complained. 'I'm...'

'You're not all right, Brendan. You just watched your father bleed to death in your arms. And with everything else on top of it, you can't expect to be fine.' She sat up and put the lamp on. 'I don't like listening to it.' She took his hand and placed it on her cheek. 'I wish there was something I could do to help you.' She turned her face into his palm and kissed it.

'You are, that's why we're here. I'm sure it'll all pass. When I accept that he's dead – and make the bastard who did it pay.'

'I hope you're right. If killing the man who killed your father brings closure, then perhaps we can get on with our lives.' She sighed. 'Or at least salvage something from what's left.'

Brendan grabbed his phone from under the pillow, beside his pistol. 'It's five thirty. We can get a few more hours sleep, then have breakfast down at the water.' He pulled Lorna closer to him and gave her a kiss. 'Thank you, for this. I'm glad I've got you by my side.'

'We're in this together, right?'

He gave her a kiss on the forehead. They both lay back down, pulling the duvet right up to their chins. It wasn't long before they drifted back to sleep again.

At seven thirty, Lorna's alarm went off. But she wasn't there to answer it. Brendan rolled over to find her side of the bed empty. Lying on his front, he strained his neck as he lifted his head to look around the room. He could hear the water running in the ensuite. He grabbed her phone and silenced it. Hearing the shower door close, he sat up in the bed, his mouth dry and his lips chapped. Biting his lips in his sleep was a bad habit he'd developed after his father was supposed to have died the first time. His psychiatrist – Dr James Harken, who'd treated Brendan for PTSD had told him it was a nervous reaction that resulted from the traumatic news of his father's disappearance. After years of counselling, the nervous biting and crying in his sleep had passed. Now, it seemed as if it had come back to haunt him.

He lay on his back, his phone suspended in the air in his line of sight. He was about to look at the news but decided against it. His focus in Italy was to take out the man who killed his father. And with Lorna's knowledge of the intelligence world, he now knew that British Intelligence's #2, now promoted to #1 assassin always went to his private home in the beautiful city of Milan, Italy. But Lake Como, where Brendan and Lorna found themselves was a simple getaway. A quiet, isolated spot where they could lay low for a few days before making their journey further south to the fashion capital. Lorna had preferred to wait longer before going after agent Max Short – the man who'd killed Brendan's father. Brendan had accepted six months. Lorna would have preferred a little longer, but Brendan was itching. He wanted Short dead the moment his father had stopped breathing.

Brendan rolled off the bed, just as he heard Lorna getting out of the shower. He could hear her humming to herself as she dried herself down. He was glad to know she was dealing with the traumatic experience of seeing her former mentor and father figure's brains splat all over their vehicle's windscreen. It was a shock to them both that the late Agent Hughes was the one who'd cooked up the entire plan, serving Brendan and Lorna as the culprits and blame for the government's corrupt plan to bring Northern Ireland backwards into it's dreadful past.

As he walked across the room, he caught a glimpse of himself in the wooden framed mirror that sat perched on top of the dressing table. He looked at himself and walked closer to it, maintaining eye contact with himself the entire time. His eyes glazed over. He felt the blood rush through his veins. He was looking at himself, but he was thinking of his father. The last breath he took was in Brendan's arms. Lorna was right, he hadn't got over it. Damien Cleary Jr was buried in Ireland, but the trauma of his passing was not.

Lorna walked out of the bathroom. 'You're up then. Get a shower and we'll go for some breakfast.' She spoke with as much spring in her voice as she had in her step. Shaking her hair dry with a towel, she sat down on the edge of the bed. She looked at him. 'You okay?'

'I will be after a shower and some coffee.' He smiled at her. Strolling across the room he made his way towards the bathroom. 'We're renting a car today and going to Milan. He's now lived six months longer than my father. That's six months too many.' He stopped at the door and looked back at her.

She was listening, but at the same time pulling on her black panties. She sat back down on the bed and fed her left arm through a matching bra strap. She looked up at him. 'Revenge is a dish best served cold, Brendan.' She stood up and walked towards the ensuite door. 'You know I'll support you, but it would be better to let him become complacent. He'll still be looking over his shoulder.'

He turned and looked at her. 'I know. You're right. But this is personal. I need to take him out. Every second he breathes while my father's dead feels like a knife is being driven into my gut.'

'Well, go and get ready. Then we can go hunting.' She blew him a kiss as she turned and closed the door.

# Chapter Two

AFTER TWO CHOCOLATE smothered croissants and a double espresso, they checked out of the hotel suite, making sure they took everything with them. Not wanting to leave a trail behind, they had decided to spend only one night in any hotel. They were now hunting down Max Short, the former #2 assassin for the British government. Short was automatically promoted to #1 after Brendan's father took out The Gent – the former #1. Now, in the intelligence world, Short was being hailed a hero for taking out the legendary Damien Cleary. But such fame and promotion meant that Short would have to accept the fact that Brendan would endeavour to level the score; to exact revenge on Short, writing himself into the archives of the dark underbelly of British intelligence.

'I could definitely live here,' Brendan said, as they strolled through the ancient city. Spectacular renaissance period architecture was everywhere. 'This is certainly a world apart from Belfast City.'

Lorna hummed. 'But the locals here would probably think Ireland is just as exotic. Well, to them anyway. Do you mind if I nip in here for a second?' She stopped him and gestured at the Roman Catholic cathedral.

Brendan didn't spend his time in any church. He thought religion had a lot to answer for. Many of the world's problems were around religion. But he was impressed the construction of this building. 'I'll wait out here.' He took a photo of her with the building in the background. 'Are you going to bring your weapon into a place like that?'

She laughed. 'Max Short wouldn't give if a shit if I was in the confession booth. I'd still get riddled with bullets.' She tapped on her handbag to indicate the gun was safely tucked inside. But would quickly be produced if needed – in a house of God or not. 'I've sent you Short's file, compliments of our friends in London. Have a look through it. And Brendan, if you want to beat this guy, you've got to stay emotionally frozen. You need a clear head.'

'I know the drill.' Brendan closed the phone's camera and went into his emails.

'Of course you do,' Lorna said, as she turned and entered the cathedral.

He stood with one foot supporting him against the exterior building's wall. When he opened the file, there he was. The man who'd killed his father. The man who was now thought of as the best in the intelligence world for taking out the man who brought new meaning the word super-agent: Damien Cleary Jr. 'Enjoy your time in Milan, because it'll be your last,' he muttered. 'Whether or not you're coming after me, rest assured, Mr Short – I'm sure as shit coming for you.'

Fifteen minutes later, at nine twenty, Lorna finally emerged from the cathedral. Her eyes puffy and red. It didn't take a genius to figure out her current emotional state.

'What is it?' Brendan asked, still leaning against the outer wall of the cathedral.

'Nothing. Just a bit emotional. That's all.' She wiped her nose with a tissue then stuffed the tissue into her handbag.

'Right, let's go buy a cheap car. Something we can ditch when we get to Milan.'

'There's a BMW dealership just a fifteen-minute walk from here. They've got a grey Mini Cooper for sale. It's on their website.'

'What do you think this is? The Italian Job?' She linked arms with him and started across the cathedral's entrance.

The sun was shining, a blinding light. But the cool air and temperature of eight degrees were enough to make the local Italians feel the pinch. Mother Nature's reminder that summer was over. For Brendan and Lorna however, the current temperature was not as bad as what would have been in England or Ireland at this time.

By the time they arrived at the dealership, they were both sweating and had taken off all their warm outer clothes, leaving only T-shirts on, which got some strange looks from the locals.

Brendan went in while Lorna stayed outside. There were still people looking for them in relation to what had taken place in Belfast and London. And with the recommendations from Brendan's late father, they had decided to stay on the run. Too much corruption lay within the government. There was too much of a risk of them being fitted up for something.

Brendan could speak a dozen languages and Italian was one of them. He was also a confident negotiator and knew a lot about cars, so he wasn't about to get swiped by the dealer who'd probably see a foreigner as an easy target.

As Brendan approached the dealer behind the desk, he regarded the Mini from the advertisement. The display on the window said *1500.00*; with millions at their disposal they could easily have afforded a brand-new Italian supercar, but discretion was going to be key to catching Short. As Damien Cleary would have said: 'There'd be no point in roaring down to Milan in a brightly coloured car that attracts about as much attention as a spaceship landing in the Milan shopping quarter.'

'Buona giornata,' the sales man was quick to say. He stood up and approached Brendan with a bright smile that matched his perfectly white shirt.

'I'll take that car, please,' Brendan said, pointing to the Mini. 'I don't need you to prepare it. I just need it to be filled with fuel and safe to drive.'

The salesman looked taken aback. Brendan was obviously more straight to the point than the guy was used to. 'Would you like to have a look around, I have a lovely BMW just came in yesterday. It's got...'

'I'm fine, thanks. I'll just pay for the Mini now. But I only have twelve hundred - cash.'

The Italian's shocked expression had returned. He broke eye contact and his pearly whites disappeared behind his lips. At the realisation that Brendan was not ready to budge on the price, he stroked his chin and looked around his shoulder as if wishing for a second negotiator.

'I'm sorry, but I'm in a hurry. Do we have a deal?' Brendan added the pressure.

The Italian's forehead began to sweat. His face reddened. He tugged on his shirt collar. 'Okay. Okay. But just because I like English people. Come, lets arrange the paperwork.'

'I'm Irish,' Brendan corrected him.

'Perfect.' The Italian, gestured for Brendan to accompany him back to his desk.

Once the transaction was complete, Brendan waited in the car park at the back of the dealership. One of the mechanics drove the Mini off the showroom floor and handed the keys over. They took off, leaving Como behind.

Lorna checked Google Maps for the best route to Milan. Via the A9, E35 and SP35, meant they would arrive in the Sesto San Giovani region of north Milan. A good spot to ditch the car.

Brendan headed west on the tree-lined Via Asiago towards the Via Fumagalli. The sloping grass verges and impressive hills of the mountainous region reminded Brendan of a dryer version of Ireland. Green in abundance. The only difference was they were on the other side of the road, which caused his focus to jump up a notch. Taking an extra moment before he committed to any manoeuvres.

He glanced at Lorna. 'Why Sesto?'

'Just like in London, it would be better to use the underground system to get us there.' Lorna spoke while fixing her gaze on her phone. 'I've just bought us day tickets.' She sighed. 'Have you familiarised yourself with him?'

'His surname's very misleading.'

Lorna laughed. 'He's a seven-foot tall string of piss.'

'Exactly.' Brendan lowered the window to let some fresh air in. That overpowering fragrance of an old car had both of them nearly choking. 'You want to stop off at Monza and test this heap of shit out on the F1 track?'

'Not really, Brendan. Maybe when Short's dead we can start having some fun.' She cleared her throat.

'Are you sure he's going to be in Italy?'

'Guys like him don't break their routine. That's what makes them so clean and hard to catch. They have order in their minds and that order comes out in everything in their lives.'

'Maybe he will change his routine. He could just wait for us to come for him, with a nice little plan to put a bullet in both of our heads.'

'That's not going to happen,' Lorna said, as a black Lamborghini Aventador roared past them. 'We should be travelling in one of those. Nothing sexier than one of those on the road.'

Brendan laughed as he pulled into a petrol station. 'Coffee?'

Lorna nodded, still looking at her phone, her gaze fallen into a more serious one than a moment ago.

He parked at pump six and shut the engine off, then looked at Lorna. 'Hey?' He crumpled up a tiny receipt and threw it at the screen of her phone. 'Hey?'

She looked up at him.

'You okay?'

'I'm fine, Brendan.' Her smile couldn't have been less authentic. 'Really, I'm fine.'

He smiled at her. 'I'll be back in a second.'

Brendan stood by the car, filling the tank back up again. Like a turtle drawing it's head into its shell, he did the same with the collar of his jumper. He saw a family wagon pull in with an Asian couple in the front and three rowdy kids in the back. The dad, who was driving pulled into the only free pump which was on the other side of Brendan's. He heard them speak in Arabic. The dad was yelling at the kids to pipe down and behave or else they wouldn't be getting their McDonald's.

Brendan laughed, feeling the fear that was running through the kids. He remembered hearing that same threat from the man who'd died in his arms a few months ago. The fuel gun clicked. The tank was full. He walked into the shop and grabbed two lattes and two double espressos. He stood in a queue of five, now the sixth person patiently waiting for the obvious new start to process the payment.

The man in front of him stood a few inches taller than Brendan's six-foot frame. He wore a navy suit that looked like he'd just been to the tailor. The man had earphones in and was involved in a debate with whoever Maria was on the other end. Brendan wasn't particularly interested in his conversation until he heard a mention of there being a lot of police around Milan city centre. The man was complaining as he had a few test drives to do in the city and wasn't happy about having so many marked cars on the street.

The suit eventually spoke to the petrol station's new recruit in a such a condescending tone that it made Brendan want to drive his head straight into the counter. The suit swiped his card and swiftly spun on his heel, just as Brendan turned and reached down into the confectionary stall. He carefully chose before lifting two bars of chocolate. He smiled at the young man who didn't look a day over eighteen and had an expression as if he was going off to war.

'You're doing a great job, don't worry about that asshole.' He spoke in Italian. He turned and watched the suit strut across the filling station. 'Guys like him think they own the place.'

The assistant thanked Brendan, while trying to contain his grin. 'Buona giornata!'

Brendan turned and swiftly made his way back to the car. Lorna climbed over into the driver's seat and started the engine, pulling up to the shop door. Brendan jumped into the passenger seat.

'He's definitely a car salesman. Got the swagger and the attitude to go with it.' Brendan laughed. 'But he's not too happy to be taking a potential customer on a test drive around Milan.'

'What do you mean?'

'Whoever he was on the phone to said there's a lot of police around Milan today.'

'That's interesting.' Lorna took her espresso and downed it in one. Handing Brendan back the empty cup, she then signalled for the latte. She took as sip of it then set the cup between her legs.

'He could be organised crime. That dealer.'

'Why?'

'Just has that untouchable swagger.'

Brendan turned and watched as the suit's silver Maserati Quattroporte increased its distance from them.

Lorna took another swig of her latte then set the cup back in between her legs. She laughed. 'This feels too much like we're re-enacting the Italian Job.' She finished her coffee and gave the cup back to Brendan.

'Here.' He handed her a pair of sunglasses as the blinding rays of sunlight pierced through the windscreen. 'Do you know this Sesto San Giovani?'

'I've driven through it before. Not much to it, but we can dump the car somewhere close to the tube.' She glanced at him. 'We'll be in the beautiful city in the next two hours.'

Brendan looked over his shoulder to the bag on the back seat. Their arsenal that was likely to disrupt the day of the public in Milan going about their daily lives. Brendan didn't care. He had a score to settle.

# About the Author

'I'm simply a guy who wanted to write his partner a book in her language, it's just got way out of hand!'

P.M. Heron was born in Belfast and spent the first 27 years of his life on Irish soil before moving to Loughborough, England to finish his study in sports management. He completed his degree in May 2012, which was, to say the least, an inspiring time to be in Loughborough. That summer, the university hosted Team Japan and Team GB for the 2012 Olympic Games in London.

At that time, he met his partner who came to England from Italy also to study sports management. Quite a summer to remember. Obviously graduating wasn't too bad either!

Later that year, he decided to teach himself to speak Italian. As a way for him to practice what he had learned, he began writing in his work diary - in Italian - and this was how he discovered a love for writing.

In March 2015, he decided to write his partner a book - in Italian - for their 3rd anniversary.

So, after 6 months, he managed to finish that book: a story titled "La Storia Della Mia Vita" which is Italian for "The Story Of My Life".

So, he fell in love with writing but didn't know how to continue. Until Sunday 11th October 2015, while talking to a friend in a leisure centre which he had been managing at the time, he came up with the idea for his first fictional series. It's simply snowballed from there!

Read more at pmheronauthor.com.

Printed in Great Britain
by Amazon

65816114R00128